Top Dog

Steve Higgs

Contents

Chapter 1

The darkness fell away with the passage of a hellfire orb, the dark red fizzing sphere screeching across the ground toward its intended target. Another followed, the face of the demon flinging them thrown into stark relief each time he formed one only to then be sucked back into black night air when they left his hands.

Ten metres from him, and in a half crouch, Zachary Barnabus straightened up when both orbs slammed into his right side, one striking the meat of his thigh, the other hitting his lower ribs.

Frowning, he said, "Can you stop doing that? It's really annoying." Turning his attention back to the young man hunkered down behind a derelict van, he was clear in his instructions. "There's half a dozen of them ... at least. I'll deal with them, but you must stay away from the red balls they throw around. That's hellfire, and if it so much as touches your skin, it will be the last thing you remember. Got it?"

"Two of them just hit you!" the young man gibbered, utter terror stealing almost all his capacity for rational thought.

Zac placed what he hoped was a reassuring hand on the kid's shoulder.

"Hi, I'm Zac. I'm going to go mess these guys up, okay? What's your name?"

Eyes as wide as saucers, the kid babbled, "Rocco."

"Well, Rocco. Stay out of sight, but keep watching for them, okay? I can't be everywhere at once and they probably won't kill you because they want you alive."

"What for?" Rocco blurted.

Another blast of hellfire smacked into Zac's right shoulder, rocking him to the side and the pain of it made him grimace. When half a second later another one struck home on his bare buttocks, he decided enough was enough.

"No time. I'll explain after. Just stay away from them. And get out from behind this van, it's a terrible hiding place." Zac looked around, pointing an arm to a pile of rubble. "When I draw their attention, get behind those rocks and if they come for you ... yell."

Final advice delivered, Zac unfolded to his full height. He was tall for a human, and when he allowed the transformation to occur, he grew even taller. Now towering a shade over seven feet his impressive wingspan ended with claws that could cut through steel. Almost black skin and glowing red eyes made him terrifying to look at, but not for the demons.

They were aware of the rumours, wild stories about a werewolf who invaded the immortal realm to rescue a little girl and in doing so absorbed enough of the death curse to also become immortal. The six demons, in Rome on a scouting party for new familiars, had no idea how it was that the shifter was still standing after being hit with hellfire, but arrogance or stupidity made them stay to fight when what they ought to have done was run.

Pivoting in the dirt to sweep his gaze through a part circle, the huge werewolf lifted a hand to point at the demons surrounding him. They were in a derelict building yard at the edge of a residential district in Rome. The ground was coated with dirt, sand, and small rocks from excavations. An old broken-down crane towered over the immediate landscape like a robot skeleton.

The demons had picked a good spot for their ambush - it was deserted. Light and sound from the local population started a street over in each direction.

Slowly, taking his time, Zachary jerked an index finger at each demon in turn.

"Eenie meenie miney moe. Catch a demon by his toe ..."

He was speaking loud enough that the demons could hear him and stunned by his blatant lack of fear, they were flicking glances at each other, each trying to see if anyone else had any idea what was going on.

Norris, the self-nominated leader of the group, had switched to collecting shifters after a botched gathering by a rival in Bremen went south because the wizard they went up against – a little girl by all accounts – was so powerful she managed to stop hellfire in mid-air. He would have scoffed at the suggestion had the report not been made by Beelzebub himself.

Shifters were supposed to be easier. Sure, they couldn't wield elemental energy to perform spells, but when the death curse failed and the two realms were plunged back together, a werewolf under a demon's control would still be a worthwhile tool.

Norris planned to have more than one and the giant beast before him was a gift he planned to offer to Beelzebub to gain favour. Or perhaps that should be he *had* planned, for now he was questioning how it was that the enormous shifter showed so little fear when outnumbered and outgunned.

To his left, Laurene asked, "What's it doing?"

It wasn't clear who the question was aimed at, so she should not have been surprised when the shifter answered.

"There's so many of you," Zac paused his selection method for a moment, "and I can't decide whose head to rip off first."

Zac went back to eenie meenie, but his comment had proven to be the final straw for Norris. Maybe the shifter could withstand hellfire or perhaps it was a trick. Either way, he was going to bring the colossal beast down and make a slave of him.

Snarling, Norris roared, "Destroy him!" as twin orbs of hellfire formed in his palms. As one, the six demons started flinging their most terrifying and powerful weapon, multiple shots found their target before Zac could move out of the way.

The source energy, taken straight from the same power that makes the earth spin, and distorted by the demons to produce hellfire, blasted Zac from his feet. Bowled backward, he tumbled like an umbrella in a storm until he fetched up against a wall.

The bricks cracked under the impact, dust and pieces of loose mortar falling to the ground around the shifter as he righted himself.

The hellfire had ceased, the demons all pausing to take stock and assuming that was it for the werewolf, but from the billowing dust, came a voice ...

"Eenie meenie ... ah, screw it. I'll just kill whoever is closest."

The second barrage of hellfire screaming across the gap between demons and shifter failed to hit him because Zac had leapt high into the air. Somersaulting gymnastically at the apex, he fell back to earth having covered more than half the distance to the nearest of the immortals.

Taking on a foe that cannot be killed would prove daunting to most, but for Zachary, somehow it just increased the fun. He didn't have to feel bad about all the horrible things he was going to do to them, and he could really get inventive too, so when he bounded the final few metres so fast his first victim had no time to react, he did precisely what he said he would.

The severed head struck the ground by Laurene's feet, making her dance back with her eyes agog.

Hellfire filled the air, but unlike the concentrated blast that knocked him down, now he was a moving target and reducing not only the number of hits the demons scored, but also the number of demons there were to fight him off.

Behind Zac, as he raked his claws across a demon's face, cutting him to the bone before eviscerating him for good measure, Azrael, the first to fall, was already healing. Sparkling light danced where his head used to be. It was reforming, the same ancient magic that made them immortal in the first place, employed now to reform his skull.

Norris backed away, continuing to launch hellfire at the impossibly unstoppable werewolf. How was it that this mortal could withstand the raw source energy when no others could? Was the story true?

Bellowing orders, Norris sent Anthony and Graylish, two lesser caste demons to intercept the shifter.

Recognising the futility of their efforts so far, he yelled, "Use elemental magic."

When Graylish flashed a confused look his way, Norris shouted, "Hit him with lightning! Blow him up from inside!"

Sending the others forward, Norris backed up a few more metres while summoning elemental energy. It crackled along and through his skin, making him feel like he was lighting up from within. The power was at the same time, both alien and familiar – he hadn't employed elemental magic in centuries. Not since he'd gained a familiar of his own to perform basic tasks.

He'd lost that familiar when a wizard – Otto Schneider – had found a way to break the bond that enslaved the humans trapped in the demon realm. Schneider escaped with hundreds of familiars, Norris' included, and like his contemporaries, he was spitting mad about it.

Mad enough to raid the mortal realm to claim a new one for himself.

Graylish, a spell readied in his right hand, called forth a conjuring of lightning to blast the werewolf – Norris sighed to see how little imagination the demon possessed, and he didn't even get to deploy the spell.

Norris watched as Graylish was cleaved in two by a road sign.

The giant werewolf had thrown it, zipping the flat steel triangle through the air like a deadly frisbee.

Norris opted for a conjuring of water, reaching out with his senses to feel the moisture within the cells of the shifter's body. Anthony was trying to delay the beast's advance, pouring elemental magic into the ground around the shifter's feet. It was a sound tactic, and the earth spell might have worked had the werewolf been less aware.

Zachary had fought elemental magicians before and could recognise the subtle differences in their spells. He was immortal, but that didn't mean getting hit with lightning didn't hurt. He'd practiced a little with Otto Schneider and had watched the German wizard conjuring spells as he practiced and refined his art.

An earth spell could bury him, and Zac knew by the time he got out, the demons would be gone, and they would have taken the kid with them. He shot a glance at the pile of rubble where he hoped the young shifter was still hiding.

Leaping into the air just as the earth beneath his feet began to shift, Zachary threw himself at the nearest demon.

Anthony's eyes widened in horror – the werewolf refused to die! It defied logic that it could survive their hellfire. Now it was able to evade elemental magic too?

The look of shock on the demon's face as Zachary plummeted toward it, arms wide and claws ready to slash was a priceless joy that brought a smile to his face. It was another good thing about the demons: no matter what he did to them, he never felt bad about it.

Toppling backward, the panicking demon drew upon hellfire, firing at almost point-blank range.

Metres away, his water spell beginning to take hold, Norris was just cranking up the energy required to freeze the werewolf into a solid ball of ice when he saw something remarkable.

In the split second before the werewolf landed on Anthony, skewering him to the dirt, a shield appeared to deflect the hellfire orbs. It was still there now, translucent and tinged with blue light as it hovered two centimetres or so beyond the shifter's left arm.

Norris blinked. He knew precisely what it was, but he hadn't seen it in over four thousand years. The werewolf was wielding a piece of the supreme being's armour. God's armour. Betrayed and murdered, it was the supreme being's death curse that tore their race from the mortal realm where they ruled over humanity. Trapped in a parallel world since that day, the earth and its people had evolved without magic in their lives.

Until recently, that is. The death curse was failing, allowing the demons to find ways into the mortal realm. It required a lot of power, but soon the curse would fail completely – they could all feel it's effectiveness dwindling – and the fight for dominion over the earth would begin.

Yet there were worrying rumours. Talk of humans who possessed enough magical power to fight back. He'd seen it himself for that matter. A tiny woman called Anastasia Aaronson had killed her master right in front of the entire demon horde and she did it using the God Sword, the most powerful weapon to have ever existed.

No mortal could touch it without instantly dying and yet she had. No mortal could survive hellfire, and yet this shifter had, and now he had a piece of the supreme being's armour in his possession. It defied everything Norris knew.

Rising from the ground, the fifth demon torn to shreds just like the four before him, Zachary focused his glare on the last of them.

The shield, called forth when he needed it by a simple act of will, vanished once more beneath his skin. He could have used it to deflect the earlier bolts of hellfire, but he found it scared the demons off if he showed his superiority too early. Where was the fun in that?

Ultimately, he was searching for Rebecca, a demon he was determined to hurt beyond anything she could imagine. Saving the kid tonight was just part of that process. Demons were not exactly predictable, but they did form patterns. They would find a place where mortals with magic – supers – were plentiful, and would attack.

Someone needed to defend against the demon incursions, and he was happy to help prevent others of his kind from being taken as slaves. Primarily though, he was out for revenge. Rebecca killed Gitta, a woman he barely knew, but had sworn to protect. Her death left behind a parentless little girl and his brain still burned with the memory.

As the other demons slowly recovered, magic knitting their shredded bodies back together, Zac stalked the last of them. The one remaining appeared to be in charge; he'd been shouting orders and had sent the others to lose first. A grin creased Zac's lips as he thought about what he could do to the last one.

The demon was conjuring, Zac could see that, but whatever he was doing didn't appear to be having any effect.

Until Zac exhaled.

It was a warm night in Italy, and he was breathing heavy from the exertion. So why was his breath coming out cold?

Worry, an unfamiliar emotion, seeped into Zac's mind as he felt his muscles tighten. He was trying to move forward and wanted to run, but his legs didn't respond the way they ought to. In an explosion of rage-filled realisation, he saw that he was being frozen and tried to fight it.

Across from him in the derelict construction yard, Norris allowed himself a moment to savour his victory. He had the werewolf. It couldn't move. The beast's face was contorted with rage and ... was it fear Norris could see?

The process would be completed in a few more seconds and he would take his prize back to the immortal realm where he would be bound to a demon as a slave. Not only that, Beelzebub would know how to separate the shield from the shifter.

What a glorious night this was! Norris imagined how he would be honoured by the leader of the demons and granted favours. He could see it all.

What he did not see was the young shifter silently coming up behind him.

Zachary wanted to shout a warning, but his mouth wouldn't work either. He was cold, though he couldn't really feel it, and it felt as if his entire body was being squeezed. His vision was going fuzzy – another new sensation.

Rocco Sifredi, bewildered by all that had happened to him in the last few months since he first shifted, had watched the enormous werewolf fight on his behalf and knew one thing – he had to overcome his fear and help.

When Norris' manipulation of a water spell took hold, Rocco saw his rescuer falter. He didn't understand what was happening, but could easily guess what would happen to him if Zac was beaten.

Grabbing a piece of rebar from the ground to then discover it had a twenty-pound hunk of concrete on the other end of the three-foot length, he hefted it and set out to do what he could.

Norris spun around at the sound of crunching gravel, but by then it was too late. The concrete smashed into his face, instead of the back of his skull where Rocco had been aiming and the water spell failed.

His hands were cut, but Rocco held tight to the rebar and swung it again, aiming this time to take the demon down for good.

That didn't happen.

The first blow stunned Norris, but the magic preventing him from ever dying was swift to heal such minor injuries.

As Rocco's makeshift weapon came down again, Norris conjured an air spell, blasting the kid from his feet to send him tumbling. He wanted to take the young shifter as a familiar of his own, but angry now, he drew on source energy to fuel fresh hellfire.

Zachary's claws plunged straight through the back of his skull, emerging from his forehead.

As the demon's temporarily lifeless body fell to the ground, Zac gave brief thought to howling, but decided it was too clichéd. Instead, he jogged to where the kid was just picking himself up.

"You ok?"

Rocco touched his head where it was bleeding.

"Not really. Those were demons, right?"

Zac nodded. "We should get you somewhere safe. Somewhere there are people. You're not homeless, are you?" Zac knew the demons and their feral creatures, the shilt, had been preying on the homeless for centuries.

Rocco got back to upright.

"No, I'm not homeless."

Chapter 2

A cross the Atlantic, sitting in his office, the global head of the Supernatural Investigation Alliance, Colt Ironbolt, thought about the name of the organisation he ran.

SIA was no longer appropriate. It had evolved as a clandestine operation, secretly following up on ever increasing reports of unexplained phenomena. It led to the discovery of magical beings and a truth the world's governments unanimously agreed had to remain a secret.

Well, that cat was well and truly out of the bag now. Not only did the entire planet know about the supernaturals being among them, there were active marketing campaigns attempting to recruit them.

An army, that was what was needed, just not a conventional one like Ironbolt had served in. A former full bird colonel, Colt Ironbolt planned to use his current command to springboard himself all the way to the White House. He could see every step he would need along the way and knew he could pull it off. All he had to do first was save the human race from being enslaved by an army of powerful demons.

Easy.

Easy for a man with an army of supernaturals, that is.

Unfortunately, he didn't really have one of those. Not yet. He had a few platoons. A battalion perhaps if he added them all together, but it was not a cohesive, organised force. They were recruiting, yes, but volunteers were sparse.

Not just in America. Oh, no. Across the globe.

The army was the brainchild of a German wizard called Otto Schneider. That was part of the problem.

Otto Schneider was a thorn in Ironbolt's side, but Colt had convinced himself to accept the German wizard's eccentricities and refusal to obey commands because he got results. The wizard had found almost half of the familiars he rescued from the demon realm, a place Ironbolt had been forced to visit briefly and never wished to see again. On top of that, Schneider had found hundreds more supernaturals.

It was something to do with being able to employ a 'second sight'. It sounded like mumbo jumbo to Ironbolt, but he knew better than to dismiss it. In the last few weeks, shifters and wizards or witches – he wasn't sure what the politically correct term for a female elemental magic user was – had arrived at the training base in Washington.

In a hastily approved executive order from the White House, Fort McNair had been repurposed. The generals were still up in arms about it, convinced, because they knew no better, that the full might of the US forces could withstand any invader.

How Ironbolt wished that were true.

Training of the supernaturals, honing their skills so they could fight the demons and hope to survive beyond the first skirmish, was being conducted by Otto's rescued familiars for the most part. They were an odd bunch to say the least.

Taken from across the globe and some of them boasting centuries of life as they resisted ageing in the demon realm, Ironbolt trusted them about as far as he could throw them. Most of them weren't even American.

Neither were the supernaturals though for that matter. Perhaps twenty percent could boast citizenship in the greatest nation on earth, but Colt read a report last night of a young girl, a teenager, from Germany, who Otto claimed was the most powerful wizard on earth.

Well, possibly the most powerful. The jury was still out on Anastasia Aaronson. She was wanted by more than a dozen nations for acts of terrorism. She had blown up buildings – some of which were major religious sites and hundreds of years old. She was definitely responsible for dozens of deaths across a slew of countries.

Otto Schneider, cursed know-it-all that he is, mocked Ironbolt's decision to pursue her. Assigning SIA agents to apprehend the woman, Ironbolt intended to wrestle her into obedience. She was a former soldier; surely she could be convinced to follow orders. Yet Schneider laughed in his face.

"She's too powerful, Ironbolt." He hated that the wizard refused to address him as President Ironbolt.

"That's why we need her. If she's not with us, then she's against us. Either way, she must be stopped."

Sniggering again, Schneider had walked away saying, "Good luck," over his shoulder.

This was how Colt Ironbolt, President of the SIA came to be considering the name of the organisation he led. They were not investigating a hidden supernatural problem any longer, they were training an army and in pursuit of a woman who might plan to destroy everything.

Ironbolt's Army was his top choice. It ensured the whole world would know his name and described precisely what it was – an army led by him.

It needed to be an army though. An army. Not just a few hundred supernaturals, but thousands. Tens of thousands. With uniforms.

Quelling his rising excitement before it could distract him, Ironbolt tapped his mouse and focused on the computer screen as it burst into life. He was going to issue an order that would change the face of his entire organisation. It was bold and would meet with questions and challenges, but leaders always pushed the boundaries – that was how great men of the past came to have their names spoken decades or centuries after they died.

He would be counted among them.

A simple order: round up the supernaturals in your area. Using the increasing demon threat as a reason to get the supers he needed off the streets, they would be forcibly recruited into his army. The world needed a force that could respond.

He, Colt Ironbolt, future President of the United States of America, was going to supply it.

Ironbolt's Army. It had such a nice ring to it.

Chapter 3

On a remote island in Scotland, Anastasia Aaronson was thinking about what she was about to do. It was a task she'd been putting off for weeks.

Daniel, the demon who first enslaved her, was trapped in Beelzebub's torture chamber suffering indescribable torment. It pained her terribly to leave him there, the thought of his unending pain keeping her awake each night. Yet she knew that going back to get him was precisely what Beelzebub wanted.

It was a trap.

She had almost two thirds of the armour now, a magical suit that made the wearer all but invulnerable to attack. Alex, a library research assistant, and arguably Anastasia's only friend in the world, was finding locations for the pieces of armour.

There were markets. Sort of.

Alex didn't always get it right, but hiding from the world in a small apartment in Italy, she was finding places for Anastasia to look. Looking though, was nowhere near as easy as it sounds. There were demons after her for a start.

The three remaining horsemen of the apocalypse hadn't come close since she killed their fourth, Martha, in Egypt, but she knew they were on her heels. It was a problem, but one to be dealt with when the time came, not worried about now.

A bigger issue existed.

The pieces of armour she sought had been hidden so long ago that no one remembered what they were. Wars came and went, empires rose and fell.

The artefacts were all buried on religious ground, generally beneath the floor of a mosque or church or other hallowed building. But those rose and fell too.

In many circumstances, where a guardian had been assigned to keep watch over it, something had occurred during the prevailing centuries. They died before passing down the mission to watch over the precious artefact, or the territory in which it was buried changed hands.

In Scotland was a church in which she hoped to find the pair of sabatons – the piece that covers the foot – but the cliff on which it was built had collapsed into the sea more than a hundred years ago and had been abandoned a century before that.

The sabatons were almost certainly lost forever, but Anastasia didn't feel like it mattered too much. She certainly didn't plan to spend a lot of time thinking about it since there was nothing she could do either way.

Had they been close, like under the water just off the coast or something, she would have been able to feel their presence, but she got nothing.

Dismissing them, her thoughts had returned to Daniel. She'd been putting off the task of attempting a rescue for too long. At least, that was how it felt.

Indecision.

If she was captured, Beelzebub would get the armour. She would effectively deliver to him the very thing that he wanted. That was the risk inherent in going back for Daniel. But Daniel was only there because he tried to rescue her. Ill-timed, Daniel's foolish rescue attempt came after the four horsemen had already taken her back to the mortal realm to search for the armour.

To help her, Daniel willingly went against everything he had previously stood for, and she had waited weeks to even attempt to free him.

"Ready?" asked Benjamin.

The angel, another outcast like Daniel, chose to lead a raid against Beelzebub when he learned the lord of demons had captured Anastasia and held in his possession the God Sword. Many angels died that day, and they achieved nothing. For that, the angels' ruler, Beelzebub's brother, Godfrey, banished him.

Anastasia drew in a deep breath before levelling a sideways grin at her companion.

"Are you?"

A laugh burst from the angel's lips. "How can anyone be ready for what we are proposing to do?"

Their hope ... their expectation, was that a small force, just the two of them, would be able to sneak into Beelzebub's house undetected. A larger force might stand more chance, but would also be discovered immediately.

There were no words left to exchange. They were either going to do it or they were not. A snort of amusement left Anastasia's nose as Yoda's words echoed in her head.

"Do or do not. There is no try."

Benjamin, the quote meaning nothing to him, shot Anastasia a curious look.

She flapped a dismissive hand in his direction – her right hand, not her prosthetic left.

"You may have missed a few things living in the immortal realm."

The time for words was done. With an exaggerated crick of her neck, a nervous gesture to make her feel more in the mood, she nodded that it was time to do what they said they would.

Stepping into Benjamin's personal space, she took hold of his right wrist – skin to skin contact was required for portal travel. Moments later, the temperature around her body shifted as she arrived back in the trees to the north of Beelzebub's grand estate.

Chapter 4

Now back in human form and clothed, Zac allowed Rocco to lead him toward the brighter streets just a short walk away. As a general principle, Zac avoided cities, they just weren't conducive to a peaceful life. People, that was the problem. Wherever there were people, there were other people willing to exploit, bully, and victimise those who were unable to defend themselves.

Zachary Barnabus had an inbuilt inability to turn a blind eye to it. If he saw the weak being subjugated, he had to act. For him that almost always meant bloodshed. So he stayed away as a rule.

He drifted mostly, moving from place to place, taking work where he could find it and keeping to himself. However, having run into one too many demons attempting to 'steal' shifters to be familiars in the demon realm, he chose to actively seek out pockets of his brethren. That it also supported his desire to find Rebecca was a welcome bonus.

Encounters with others like him had been rare. His entire life, he'd only met a handful of other shifters, but in the last few months that had changed, and more and more were announcing their true selves.

He knew why.

The world had changed.

He grew up in the shadows, hiding his true form and running away from home and all he knew lest he destroy it. Now Ayla Pendragon, a high-ranking woman within the SIA, was all over the internet and social media assuring the world that it was okay to be a supernatural. She was encouraging them to put their hands up and be counted for the world needed them.

So Zachary left Croatia where he'd stumbled across a small enclave of shifters in Mostar. There, he'd fought demons and their pets, killing dozens of shilt, and pummelling the demons. It was there that he had gained the shield.

An old priest gave it to him. The war that raged there in the nineties had rained destruction on the city, and the cathedral had suffered terrible damage. The old priest wasn't even sure which side to blame, but a whole section of a wall was destroyed and priceless, centuries-old stained-glass windows reduced to rubble in a single moment.

In the rubble, they had found a box. It had been hidden inside a column, the hollow compartment unknown and unseen for too many generations for it to be remembered. A verger had opened it, dying the instant he reached inside to touch the shield that lay within.

When Zachary arrived, fighting demons and saving the old priest's parishioners in the process, he had heard the shield calling to him. Warned not to touch it with the story of what happened to the last mortal who tried, Zachary offered a glib comment and picked it up.

The shield bonded with him, anchoring to his soul, and vanishing as if it had never been. Its physical form ceased to be, only to return when he was threatened, or he called it forth. It had taken some getting used to, but he liked it.

With traffic increasing around him, Zac fought against the discomfort he felt.

"You said it wasn't far," he reminded Rocco, his words a thinly veiled warning.

The young shifter, new to his ability and still coming to terms with all that it meant, spun around to walk backwards a few paces. With a grin on his face, he pointed.

"That's my father's bar. Well, actually, I suppose it's my grandfather's bar, but my father runs it now. One day it will be mine, I guess."

The place Rocco indicated was across the street and about fifty metres away.

Zachary steeled himself. He did not do well in group environments unless the people were friendly.

They usually weren't.

Rocco acted as if he hadn't almost been abducted by demons ten minutes ago. The nearer they got to the bright lights ahead, the more animated and excited he became. He was almost dancing when he reached the bar's entrance.

Following his new 'friend' through the door, Zachary found all eyes swinging his way. Was it because he had to duck to get through the door? Did his scruffy clothes and backpack over one shoulder make them stare?

At the bar, Rocco was already engaged in conversation with a man who had to be his father so similar were their features. The younger man leaned right over, his feet off the floor and speaking loudly so the older man would hear above the hubbub of conversation.

Zachary tracked his eyes from left to right, meeting the gaze of anyone and everyone looking his way. It amounted to more than half the people in the bar.

Rocco's father was already coming his way, flipping a section of the bar upward to escape its confines. Rocco met him, and still smiling like the Cheshire cat, walked with his father all the way to stop a scant foot from Zachary.

Zac looked down at the father. He didn't have to look down as far as he did with most men, Rocco's father had to be a metre ninety five tall and he was broad. Under normal circumstances Antonio would be considered a large man. His chest and arms were thick with muscle. The kind that one gets from time in the gym, not that formed by a hard working life.

Zac assessed that the man was probably a boxer in a younger version of his life. A fighter of some kind for sure. It was the way he held himself that gave it away – poised, ready to react and his eyes constantly on the move as he watched Zachary for any indication he might make a move.

Despite the muscle, Rocco's father was soft around the middle and a little doughy in general, but a big man, nonetheless.

"I understand you saved my boy."

"I was in the right place at the right time," Zac replied noncommittally, and saw the skin around Rocco's father's eyes tighten.

"That's not how my boy tells it. He says you showed up right when they were going to take him. He says you came out of nowhere."

Sensing that he was being challenged and not liking it one bit, Zac leaned his head down to get into the father's face.

"Oh, yeah? What else does he say?"

Rocco touched his father's arm.

"Dad, what's going on? Zac saved me. They were demons. I ..."

Rocco's father lifted a hand, a single index finger extended. It was enough to silence his son.

Zac had seen enough to judge what was occurring. Nodding his head, he drew back to his full height and crossed his arms.

"Let me guess. You're the alpha around here." The remark was aimed at Rocco's father, and it was tantamount to a challenge.

Around the immediate vicinity of the bar, men and women were getting to their feet. They'd heard what the newcomer had said, and they knew what it meant.

Bored already, Zac raised his voice.

"I am not here to challenge. My name is Zachary Barnabus, and my only desire is to help you. Demons are coming. They want you as familiars. Humans are coming too. The Supernatural Investigation Alliance wish to recruit you. They will use your abilities for their own gain."

Coming forward another pace, Rocco's father cracked a smile.

"And you're here to save us from them all?"

Rocco tried to interrupt again.

"Dad, wha ..."

This time, his father allowed the change to begin, twisting to snarl at his son and making him cower.

Zac yawned. "Yeah, you're the alpha. I find it odd that the moment two werewolves get together they immediately have to figure out who the top dog is. Why is that? Too many films on the subject that all say this is how it is?"

Rocco's father's face had returned to normal, the red that filled his eyes for a moment dimming to leave them as they were, but everyone in the bar had seen it and no one had reacted.

Zac nodded his head. They were all pack members.

Looking up at Zac's face, Rocco's father said, "My name is Antonio Siffredi. I thank you for saving my son, but this is my pack and there is no place for you here. Rocco should not have brought you." He flicked a glare at Rocco before looking back at the man filling the doorway to his bar.

Unbidden, others were drifting toward the door, pack members, both men and women, coming to back their alpha.

Arriving at Antonio's shoulders, they used their numbers to intimidate the newcomer and force him from the bar, a man with thick, frizzy black hair demanded, "What makes you think more demons will come?"

Zac waited before responding, letting his eyes rove across those looking up at him.

"Because they always do. I have experience with them."

Antonio grumbled. "If the demons come here looking for us, the pack will handle them."

His supporters were about to agree when Zac snapped. "Your pack will die." He said the words with force and conviction, lowering his voice only a little when he added, "Any mortal that stands against them is either killed or taken back to the demon realm as a slave. They are here to gather new familiars."

His words were casting doubt, and around the room, Zac could see worried glances being exchanged.

Antonio was not in the mood to listen.

"If that is true, how is it that you fought them tonight? You say no mortal can stand against them, yet according to my son you took on six and beat them all. Are you going to claim that you are immortal?" He made a joke of it and got the ripple of laughter he wanted in response. "There is just one of you and more than forty of us. I think we will be able to protect ourselves."

Taking the shortest route to the solution, Zachary flexed his left forearm and with the motion brought the shield to life. More than half those pressed in close to him jumped back, unable to hide their surprise though Antonio managed to resist flinching.

Zac growled into the alpha's face, "I don't have the patience to argue with you. You think I'm here to challenge you? I'm not. I was able to beat the demons because I went to the demon realm with a wizard and came back enhanced." Admitting he was immortal would just make them want to challenge it and distract them from what he wanted to achieve. "News of demon incursions is all over the news. They gravitate toward hotspots, usually following the shilt. The shilt prey on the homeless population; those who will not be missed, only moving on when they meet resistance, usually in the form of supernaturals."

"The shilt?" The question came from a woman. Short and lean, she came to stand beside Rocco just a metre or so behind the alpha. It was obvious she was Rocco's mother and thus almost certainly Antonio's wife. The pack beta.

Zac didn't want to get into it, just as he didn't want to admit that the reason he gave for being there wasn't the whole truth. Yes, he did want to prevent the demons from taking more familiars, and yes, he had spent his whole adult life alone because he was dangerous to people. Being part of a pack was attractive, yet he knew he could never join one because his size and strength dictated that they would look to him to lead. He had no interest in that.

He'd been looking for Rebecca, and having drawn a blank, was ready to move on.

To explain as briefly as possible, Zac said, "Nasty things from the immortal realm that feed on life force. They use a charm to disguise their form, so they look just like regular people when they enter the mortal realm. They can kill too, but they probably wouldn't chance their army with a werewolf because they are not that hard to kill."

Antonio was about to say something and snarled when Zachary talked right over the top of him.

"You can choose to ignore me; I hold no sway over you. There is a war coming, you've all seen it on the news," Zac lifted his eyes to look over the alpha's head, further angering him. "This is not about picking sides; you will get no choice in the matter. If you can avoid them until then, so much the better. Stay together," Zac aimed the comment and his gaze at Rocco. "Don't wander off by yourself and you might be safe."

He held the attention of the bar for a few seconds more, meeting the eyes of as many as possible before turning around and leaving without another word.

Walking away, his steps unhurried, Zac counted in his head. He was at eight when Antonio kicked the bar door open.

Chapter 5

S neaking around in the devil's palace, could there be a dumber thing to do? Okay, so Beelzebub wasn't really the devil, not in the way that the Bible portrays him, but the ruler of the demons wanted to subjugate humanity and rule over them, so the differences in the truth and the half-remembered legend were relatively insignificant.

Benjamin opened a portal inside the grand house, a feat only possible because he'd seen inside it when he led the raid. With an almost inaudible pop, the portal snapped shut behind him. This had been one of the riskiest parts of the rescue attempt: getting inside Beelzebub's house undetected. It was just after ten at night when he and Anastasia left Scotland, and because Beelzebub's house was geographically located in the South of England in the mortal realm, it was also just after ten there.

It would have been nice to have opened a portal directly inside Beelzebub's torture room located in the sub level beneath his house. However, Benjamin and Anastasia agreed there was too much of a risk that there would be someone other than Daniel inside the room.

To that end, they picked a room in a dark corner at the edge of the building. Pausing for a moment to get their bearings and to listen for anyone who might have heard their arrival, they held their collective breaths.

Anastasia's heart thumped in her chest, not for fear of being caught and what might happen afterward, but for the risk she was taking with the armour and the demon killing weapon she carried. Discovered in Egypt, the throwing knife, a short, wide dagger attached to a magical silver chain could be thrown and recalled to her hand. By pushing source energy through it once it was embedded in the body of a chosen victim, Anastasia could kill a demon.

The ability to wield the weapon came from a skill unique to her and just two others that she knew of – she could sustain a stream of source energy. Demons and angels alike could form the earth's primal energy into orbs to be flung, but she could fire it like a water cannon and that enabled her to kill a race previously thought to be immortal.

She fingered the weapon now for security, holding the hilt of the dagger and ready to throw if the need arose.

Anastasia was certain it would.

"Which way?" she whispered, wanting to move, yet uncertain which direction she needed to go. The mansion was a sprawling beast of a house and she had only been there for a short time previously before Beelzebub sent her away with the four horsemen.

Benjamin pointed rather than speaking, keeping the noise they made to a minimum. The recent angel incursion, led by Benjamin and ultimately flawed because they were so badly outnumbered, had to have made the demons more wary. Would there be guards?

It felt safe to assume so.

They crept through the house, stealing toward the stairs that led down to the basement. Dungeon might be a better name, Anastasia considered. In other times in human history, that was exactly what it would have been called.

In the dead of night, they encountered no one, arriving back in the same room Benjamin had left Daniel in so many weeks ago. He'd told the demon he would be right back, a foolish statement based on hope and good intentions.

Rounding the door, her eyes wide as she looked for him, Anastasia was unable to stifle her gasp when she spotted him.

Sandwiched between two metal plates that kept his body in place, he was impaled in more than a dozen places where spikes in the top plate protruded through holes in the bottom. Set at a forty-five-degree angle so Daniel's head was uppermost and facing down, she had to come around to the front and crouch to get her face in line with his.

The demon was unconscious, but as she drew closer, a shaking hand to her mouth, his eyes fluttered open.

"Daniel," she managed to utter his name, horrified by what she was seeing and wishing it wasn't showing in her eyes.

He looked at her, recognition taking a moment to catch on, then his eyes flicked across to take in Benjamin.

Parodying the angel's voice, he said, "I'll be right back. You dick."

With a frown, Benjamin offered a retort. "We can just leave you here, if you like. Maybe come back next month instead."

Ignoring their banter, but pleased Daniel's mind hadn't gone to mush through the countless hours of torment, Anastasia asked, "How do I open this ... thing?"

If the device had a name, she had no idea what it was, but only a twisted mind could have devised it.

Unable to move his head more than a few centimetres, Daniel had to use his eyes to indicate direction.

"There's a handle on this side. It takes source energy to open it."

With quiet steps, she made her way around the machine.

"Here?"

Employing an impatient tone, Daniel said, "I can't see what you are touching, can I, Ana? Good grief. You leave me here all this time, and then want my help to open a torture device I am trapped inside."

Resisting the urge to wallop him, not that she could get to much of his body with the machine encasing him, she found what looked to be a handle and gripped it.

Raw source energy coursed through her body, forming in her chest as it always did to crackle outward into her arms. Her left, prosthetic hand, until recently unable to do what she could with the right, was now able to channel magic and use it due to the gauntlets she found in pursuit of God's suit of armour.

Holding a sustained stream of sinfire, the angels' purer and less harmful version of the demons' weapon, and the one her body was able to produce for itself, she attempted to unlock the device.

Nothing happened.

"What's happening?" asked Daniel, straining his neck muscles to see though all he succeeded in doing was banging his skull against the upper steel plate.

"It's not working," Anastasia remarked, trying to work the problem in her head. "You told Benjamin it needs a sustained stream to open it, right? Are you sure this thing isn't coded so only Beelzebub can release whoever is in it?"

Daniel tried to shrug. "I was conscious when they forced me in here. He bragged that only he could ever set me free because it had been engineered to need a sustained stream of hellfire …"

"Hellfire," Benjamin repeated, hitting the nail on the head.

"What?" Daniel craned his neck the other way to hook an eyebrow at the angel. "She isn't using Hellfire?"

"No," Anastasia moaned. "I can't produce it, remember?"

"Well, I can't see what you are doing, can I? Useless mortal." Daniel's tone was that of an employer looking for people to fire. "So, what now?"

Anastasia bowed her head, sucked in a deep breath, and looked up.

"Now, I guess I'm off to pick a fight."

Chapter 6

Finding someone to fight proved harder than expected. Leaving Daniel in the dungeon, Anastasia and Benjamin roamed the halls to seek out a demon.

It seemed ironic that they had been so worried about encountering overwhelming odds and now they were deliberately seeking a demon there were none to be found.

"Surely, there has to be at least one demon around here somewhere?" Benjamin complained. He was going to say something else, but a fresh thought had found its way into Anastasia's head, and she placed a hand over his mouth to silence him once more.

"The sword."

Two words that carried more than enough meaning. She didn't need to explain; Benjamin instantly understood what she was suggesting.

"It will be with him," he warned.

Her reply was a surprise even to her. "It's more important than Daniel."

She wanted to rescue the demon. She believed she owed him for what he had done for her. What he had tried to do, but she couldn't put him before the rest of the human race. With the God Sword in his possession, Beelzebub became unstoppable. Without it … well, the jury was still out on whether humanity could do anything to stop him, but since she was one of only three beings known to be able to wield it, she felt a lot safer with it in her hands than anyone else's.

Benjamin nodded, accepting her opinion without argument.

"We'll have to find his chambers."

Anastasia started walking. "No need. I've been there before."

It took a moment to orientate herself, but once she found the grand staircase leading upward, she knew she could find where the master of all demons slept.

Assuming he was asleep, that is. Assuming he was even here and not elsewhere. He could be in the mortal realm wreaking havoc for all she knew.

Staying silent and sticking to the shadows as best they could, they crept through Beelzebub's mansion, she stopped outside a door.

"This is it?" Benjamin hissed, his whisper too quiet to be heard by anyone other than Anastasia.

Ana paused, her hand hovering above the door handle.

"I think so." The question of whether she had the right door or not was not the one bothering her at that moment. She was too busy questioning whether she ought to have sinfire ready to fling or if the light from it would wake the sleeping ruler of hell if he was indeed inside.

There was only one way to find out. Playing the cautious card, she held a connection to her source of energy but didn't power herself up. Not just yet.

Slipping around the door and praying it wouldn't creak loudly, she held her breath as it swung open. Paused in the doorway to listen for signs of life, she recognised the room inside. Though it was dark now with very little light coming from windows to her right, she knew the layout. Beyond the room she was walking into was the demon lord's bedroom.

A noise made her freeze and when Benjamin failed to spot her lack of forward movement in the dark, he bumped her arm and made her jump.

It was no good; she just couldn't see and there was no way to find the sword without light.

Producing an orb of sinfire in her right hand, while keeping her left on the hilt of her throwing knife, Anastasia advanced across the shadowy room.

She didn't get very far.

The sound of someone – someone large – throwing themselves out of bed with a trumpet of rage filled the air. That she was hearing Beelzebub was never in question. What to do now, that was the one at the top of the decision tree.

Yanking her knife from its scabbard to hold it aloft and ready to throw, she ran toward the bedroom's entrance.

Benjamin shouted something, but the words were lost in the heat haze of neurons firing in her brain. Adrenalin took over. She had brought the fight to the lord of hell and now she had to win or lose everything. Including her life.

Dark red light - hellfire being formed - illuminated the walls just as she ran into the bedroom. Expecting to find Beelzebub, Anastasia froze for a half second when she found two female demons in his bedchamber too.

They were naked, but armed with hellfire. Failing to react swiftly enough worked in her favour for the women threw their orbs her way. Beelzebub had almost done the same before he saw who it was.

His shout of, "No!" came too late and Anastasia revelled in the blast of energy she received when all four hellfire orbs struck home. The first time she'd ever been hit with it, the energy contained within tore her from the ground, launching her hundred-pound frame across the kitchen of her tiny flat. Now, she was able to absorb it the moment it touched her body.

Charged up and ready to free Daniel, Anastasia now faced the challenge of getting back to him.

Whipping out her right arm, she launched the throwing knife like a deadly missile. Aimed right for Beelzebub's chest, Ana's heart sank when he neatly sidestepped it.

"You dare to enter my house?" Beelzebub roared.

Benjamin fired over her head, twin orbs of sinfire, less potent and less deadly than the demon's twisted manipulation, it was nevertheless powerful enough to pulverise the female demon they struck.

There was no sign of the sword, but Ana couldn't believe it would be far from Beelzebub at any point.

The demon lord advanced, unwilling to use hellfire on Anastasia, but no less deadly for it, he was conjuring elemental magic.

With Benjamin trading blows with the one female demon still on her feet, Anastasia could focus on Beelzebub, but she knew they had only seconds before more demons would arrive. The knife had returned to her hand, the thread of silver retracting so she could throw it again and this time she launched an orb of hellfire from her left hand in a bid to make her target dodge into her line of fire.

It worked, the knife plunging into Beelzebub's muscular core. Unable to believe her eyes, Anastasia poured source energy into the weapon. She could kill him! She could kill the master of hell right now!

"Ana! We have company!" Benjamin's bellow broke through her fog of concentration. She had Beelzebub. In moments he would be dead, yet no sooner did she think that than the demon reached inward to pluck the knife from his body.

Her sustained stream of energy continued to flow between them, but now, with the knife clenched in his right hand, he pushed his own magic back at her.

It was a battle of wills and his will proved stronger.

Hellfire coursed into her body, surging from the thread of silver and up her arm to overload her synapses. In an instant, her brain felt like it was on fire.

Beelzebub leered at her, coming closer as he stalked across the bedroom.

Behind her, Benjamin was fighting someone new; more demons *had* arrived. They needed to go, and they had to do it right now. Trying to get the sword had been foolish. It wasn't as if she had any idea where he kept it.

An orb of sinfire, shot by her face, Benjamin finding a second to launch a blast at Beelzebub. The demon flicked it away as one might a bothersome fly.

Were her eyes going to explode in her skull? They felt like they might. Attempting to fight against the energy being pushed into her, she was losing. Stars began to dance at the periphery of her vision, but she saw when Beelzebub nodded his head at one of the female demons he'd been with. They were both on their feet again, Benjamin's best attempts to improve their odds having only temporary success.

Anastasia didn't recognise either of them, but she understood Beelzebub just demanded they both stand down. Neither was attempting to take any further part in the fight, allowing their master to demonstrate his superiority.

"Jomana, if you please?" Beelzebub addressed the one to his left, inviting her cordially without a need to state what it was that he wished for her to do.

Now though, he wanted something, and with a jolt, Anastasia realised what it was.

Jomana walked across the room, acting oblivious to the battle raging just a few metres from her. At a wardrobe, she stopped to open the doors and reach inside.

Anastasia readied herself and when the naked female demon withdrew the God Sword, she acted.

Dropping any resistance to Beelzebub's dominant display of source energy mastery, she also dropped the throwing knife. The handle tumbled to the floor, disconnecting the flow of magic overloading her body. She staggered, but was already shouting.

"Benjamin! A portal!"

It was going to be a split-second thing. It would either work or they were both dead.

Grabbing a tight hold of Benjamin's robe, she ran for the demon with the sword. She had to cover two metres, that was all.

Startled, the sudden change in tactics catching her by surprise, Jomana almost dropped the sword as she automatically tried to form fresh hellfire to defend herself.

Beelzebub roared, darting across the room as the swiftest method to stop what was about to happen.

Caught in a moment of indecision, Jomana raised the God Sword. It was too late for Anastasia to alter her trajectory, but she managed to sweep an arm up to parry the tip of the blade as it swung toward her throat.

Slamming into her, Anastasia screamed, "Now!" The sword cut into the skin by her left ear, the sting of it like fire inside her flesh. Falling toward the carpet, the portal opened under them, and they fell through, Beelzebub's bellows of rage following.

At the last second, Benjamin out of control and spinning where his body had been dragged off balance by Anastasia's rough grip, snagged the trailing end of the discarded throwing knife and the dagger whipped through the closing portal just as it snapped out of existence.

Chapter 7

"There is no need for you to do this." Zac's words were heard by half the pack, Antonio's extended family had followed him out into the street. "There is nothing to gain by it." Even as he said the words, he knew there was going to be no reasoning with the alpha. Antonio's face told a story that anyone could read.

"You come into my place and disrespect me?" Antonio challenged. He felt undermined, the giant shifter returning his son with a tale of being saved from a gang of demons was bad enough – it was the alpha's job to keep the pack safe. Maybe that could have been tolerated, but the stranger talked down to him, addressing Antonio's pack as if *he* were the voice of authority.

He'd never had to fight to claim his place as pack leader; no one stood to challenge him and as bar owner, he was already in a position where others gravitated toward him. He was the linchpin in the community and no newcomer was going to have the last word.

Chasing after his father, Rocco tried again to reason with the patriarch.

"Dad, I've seen him fight. You can't beat him."

Zachary sighed. In that one sentence, the kid had sealed his father's fate. Now there was no way for Antonio to back down.

Of course, there had never been any intention of letting the stranger walk away; Antonio wanted to fight the giant. Beating a younger man: a muscular, taller, younger man, would cement his position in the minds of all pack members, now and for the future. They would talk of this fight for years to come. Sure, the stranger was undoubtedly strong, but Antonio was confident in his ability as a fighter.

First, he had to deal with his son's comment.

He hadn't laid a hand on his son in years. Not since he was a small boy and Antonio caught him sneaking candy from the larder. Whipping around, he delivered a backhanded blow to Rocco's face.

The whip-crack sound of it shocked everyone. So too did the flying form of Rocco who fell backward to sprawl on the sidewalk. There was blood coming from his bottom lip.

Until then, Zachary had been sympathetic toward the pack leader; his intention only to move on. Now he wanted to make a point.

The pack had fanned out to either side of Antonio just as they did in the bar. Their expressions were a mix of curiosity and excitement. The stranger was five metres away, standing in the street where he glared back at their alpha.

"Where?" Zac growled. He intended to find a spot where they would not be seen, a loading yard behind the businesses or something. Antonio had other ideas.

With a snarl, the bulky former fighter drove off with his right foot, running at Zac as he ripped off his shirt. "How about right here!" he raged as the transformation changed his body.

There were cars moving past them in the street, mid-evening traffic on their way to somewhere. The motion of Antonio running drew more than one eye, and when those eyes saw the man become a werewolf there was nothing to stop the inevitable crash that followed.

Zachary resisted the temptation to also transform. It wasn't as if he believed he needed the advantage that came with it. As a werewolf Antonio would be faster and stronger than before. He was taller too and his arms were longer. Now tipped with long claws that would be razor sharp, he was deadly to a mortal and could kill another shifter just as easily. Not only that, his skin, the tone of it now dark like charcoal, was harder and less easy to penetrate.

Staying in mortal form was the point.

Zachary was going to beat the alpha without even needing to transform: an ultimate insult.

In the street to Zac's left, cars ploughed into cars. Horns blared as metal crunched and panicked people shouted and screamed their horror and fear.

Oblivious to the mayhem, Antonio rushed his opponent, proving his lack of experience – boxing isn't fighting, it's a sport. Running at Zachary, his arms up to show his claws, he was unable to alter his trajectory when his opponent ducked, swivelled and swept out a leg to chop away his feet.

Tripped, Antonio did his best to control his fall, but could not avoid hitting the deck. Converting his momentum into a roll, he bounced back to his feet in a move that Zachary considered athletic for a bigger man.

That didn't stop him whipping out a long right leg to kick the alpha in his teeth.

Shunted back, his head snapping all the way to one side, Antonio wobbled but did not go down.

"You shouldn't have hit your son," Zachary chose to make a point. "He was right, you can't beat me. Listening to him would have saved you from this situation."

Antonio screeched in rage, announcing his charge like a complete amateur before he set off again.

Zachary feigned a retreat, a fast step back that allowed him to launch forward in a course correction that caught the alpha by complete surprise. A sweeping arm knocked Antonio's claws to one side before they could find flesh, and a jackhammer punch to the gut doubled him over.

Backing off a pace, and telling himself to consider it done, Zac sucked in a deep breath before turning to face the rest of Antonio's pack.

Should he apologise? Should he check on Rocco; the kid had taken quite a blow from his father? Maybe this was the time to reinforce his message about the demons.

He got to do none of those things for as he started to open his mouth, he saw the faces looking back at him shift their gaze.

Antonio should have known when enough was enough, but he didn't. Zac had gone easy on him and that was a mistake.

Spinning to deliver another blow – one that would put the alpha down and end the fight – Zac discovered he was already too late.

A wild swinging arm raked across his face, ripping through the flesh on his forehead and continuing down through his eyebrows, nose, cheeks, and lips.

Reeling from the blow, Zachary heard the pack gasp as his blood flew.

Antonio could have … should have followed up with further strikes to press home his brief advantage, but the alpha believed the injury he'd just inflicted was all he needed.

In full view of the now baying crowd, Zachary staggered back a pace. Through the blood flowing over his ruined face, he checked his opponent, found Antonio to be grinning victoriously, and folded his arms in a nonchalant manner.

His casual attitude silenced the pack, a hush spreading through them as uncertainty froze the look on their alpha's face.

Right before their eyes, the giant stranger's face was healing. The blood had stopped flowing, and the skin was knitting itself back together. The gashes deep into his flesh closed and when it was done, Zachary pulled up the bottom of his blood-stained t-shirt to pat his face dry.

The blur of motion that followed was hard for the human eyes to track, yet even though Zachary felt confident he could kill Antonio with a single blow, he still held back, pulling his punch so it collapsed the man's windpipe but didn't rupture it.

There wasn't a sound in the street. The crashed cars had blocked the lanes in both directions, and though terrified by what they were seeing, the drivers and passengers had fallen silent to watch the fight. Many had left their vehicles to get a better look.

Zachary gave the pack a final look and walked away. This time, no one followed him.

Chapter 8

Ana's eyes bored into Jomana's as they fell. They both gripped the sword, however her position at the bottom of the pile dictated that it was Jomana who hit the ground first.

The air went from her lungs and her grip faltered. It was all Anastasia needed.

Of course, she hadn't factored in Benjamin who chose that precise moment to slam into her back. With a whoosh, her breath rushed out and she too lost control of the deadly weapon pinned between her and the demon.

Sucking in a lungful of air, Anastasia swore when yet again the ground fell away beneath them. Benjamin had opened another portal. Or Jomana had. Anastasia couldn't know for sure until they slammed into the floor a half heartbeat later.

They were back in the dungeon, precisely where they needed to be. It meant Benjamin had controlled their movement, but it was hardly time for jubilation. Not when she was on the floor in a tangle of limbs, struggling for breath, bleeding from a wound to her head, and in danger of getting skewered.

Benjamin's second impact had thrown Ana to one side and spat Jomana free. The sword lay between them, and the demon was faster to react.

With a snarl of panicked rage, Jomana snatched up the weapon and rolled away.

Anastasia heard it clatter on the stone floor as the demon put distance between them. Driving off the floor on wobbly legs, she faced her opponent.

The terrible torture device with Daniel trapped inside was behind Jomana. She had to go through her to get to him.

"Daniel! I'm coming!" Anastasia cried, hoping that would be true. Still charged up with hellfire, if she got the chance, she could free him.

Jomana screamed, a mix of fear and challenge.

"In the dungeons! We are in the dungeons!"

They had seconds, nothing more.

The terrified demon thrust the sword, aiming to kill Anastasia right there and then, and she might have succeeded were Anastasia not protected by a magical suit of armour. Parrying the thrust with her left arm, the blow struck against a vambrace where it covered her elbow. Invisible until it was needed, the armour appeared above Anastasia's skin like a glowing blue forcefield.

The sight of it stunned Jomana and that was all the opportunity she got. Benjamin, just clambering to his feet, threw Anastasia's dagger to score a direct hit. Unlike Anastasia, the angel couldn't push source energy through the weapon to kill Jomana, but with the dagger lodged in her throat, the female demon dropped the sword to claw at her wound.

"Portal!"

Benjamin's cry of warning jolted Anastasia into action. Whipping the sword from the ground, she ran three paces to drive it through the opening portal. Demons were trying to come through, abandoning caution to obey their leader's commands.

The cry of agony was followed by the portal closing again, but another was already appearing on the other side of the room. There was no way to defend their position. All she could do was attempt to free Daniel and hope Benjamin could buy her the time to do it.

Pushing her body to do more than it felt capable of, she ran to the torture device. It was facing away from where their portal had dumped them, so Daniel couldn't see anything that had happened.

"Was that Jomana?" he asked, his voice hoarse. "I hate that bitch."

Anastasia didn't answer. With the sword in her left hand, she gripped the device's handle with her right. Demons were arriving in the room, and though they were bottlenecked as they tried to step through their portals, they would overpower Benjamin in a heartbeat.

Focusing to hold a sustained stream of hellfire, she expected to have to fight the machine, but the handle moved the moment she pushed against it. The device unlocked, the top plate swinging up and out of the way, taking the spikes with it.

No longer pinned in place, Daniel slid out, the angle of the machine encouraging gravity to do its job, but any hope Anastasia held that Daniel might help them fight faded when he collapsed into a pool of his own blood. His body folded upon itself; his muscles unable to support his weight after weeks trapped unmoving inside the machine.

Snapping her head up to bark at Benjamin – they needed a portal back to the mortal realm right now – she saw the forlorn look on his face.

Demons from more than half a dozen portals were pouring into the room and in the instant their eyes locked, Benjamin was hit by so many blasts of hellfire, it hurt her eyes to look.

Hunkered down on the floor behind the machine, Ana grabbed Daniel's left hand.

"You have to open a portal, Daniel. Open it now or go back in the machine."

He didn't act as if he had even heard her, but his fingers twitched and the floor they were lying on suddenly wasn't there.

Chapter 9

F alling rather than stepping through a portal was always a jarring experience, but bracing herself for the impact she felt sure was coming, she failed to anticipate that she would land in water.

The cold shocked her just as much as finding herself submerged. Flailing for a second and trying to keep a hold of Daniel's limp form, she struggled to hold her breath. Daniel was beneath her, his face fully submerged, not that she could see him properly it was so dark.

It was a fight to get her head back to the surface. Until her hand touched a solid surface that is, and her fingertips reported the feel of manufactured tile just beneath her backside. Kicking out a leg, she got a foot down to the floor and found she could stand up.

The water was only waist deep.

"Oh, my God," she blurted, the unmistakable silhouette of Nelson's Column towering above her to remove any ambiguity regarding where she was. Swinging her head around to check the National Gallery was where she expected it to be, she marvelled to find she was in Trafalgar Square in the heart of London.

"Must rest," Daniel mumbled, his head above water where Anastasia held it. Before she could speak, the demon opened another portal and again they fell down through it.

This time they fell harder and landed on grass. Water from the fountain came with them. Splashing down and washing outward, it soaked into the soil. They were back in the immortal realm, not that Anastasia recognised where they were. She didn't need to in order to know that was where they had to be – the portals went between the realms. To get from one place in the mortal realm to another one had to return to the home of the demons.

Fortunately, the immortal realm is a vast and largely unpopulated place.

With a yelp of shock, Ana felt the ground beneath her fall away yet again. She wanted to shout at Daniel, yet she knew he couldn't stand so they could walk through the portals he was opening.

A grunt of pain from Daniel echoed Ana's thoughts on the matter and she said, "We're safe now. Can you stop doing that?"

He didn't move, his body still looking like a crumpled heap, but he said, "One more."

She opened her mouth to protest, but the portal he opened this time was perpendicular to the ground and she could walk through it. Not only that, what she could see on the other side looked like a hotel room. Not just any hotel room, but a plush suite.

Assuming it was safe to enter, she trapped the sword under her left arm, grabbed Daniel's collar and heaved him through the portal. It closed behind her, and she finally felt herself relax.

Until she remembered Benjamin. She left him there. She left him to replace Daniel inside that awful torture device. Was he already being loaded into it?

Not that there had been anything she could have done about it, and truthfully, she would have sacrificed him by choice if she needed to. The armour and the sword were too important to allow them to fall into anyone else's hands. She had them now. The throwing dagger too.

Pushing the guilt she felt over Benjamin from her mind, Ana looked down at Daniel and lowered herself to sit on the edge of the bed. She was exhausted. How long had it been since she'd eaten?

There was a bed and there had to be the option of food. Not that she had anything as simple as a credit card with her, and whatever room they were staying in, they hadn't booked so it wasn't like they could order room service.

Dirty, smelly, battered, and reaching up to touch her neck, she added covered in her own blood to the list, she needed to take a pause and tend to some of her basic needs. It was that or risk collapsing.

She would rest. A few hours, that was all she needed. Just a few hours.

There was no conscious decision to lie down, but when she awoke hours later, she was shocked to find it was still dark outside and Daniel's sleeping form was in the bed next to her.

Clawing at her stomach when it rumbled, she rolled out of bed and stopped.

"Where the hell are my clothes," she blurted, her voice a startled hiss as she stared down at her bare legs and torso. The only item she still wore were her knickers. Daniel had recovered enough to clamber into bed, and she had been so out of it that she didn't even notice him stripping off her clothes.

What else did he do?

The shocking question reverberated inside her skull for a few seconds before being dismissed. *That* she would have woken up for.

Her prosthetic arm and foot were on the nightstand – he'd removed those too and next to them was a tube of the cream she used to soothe the skin on her stumps. That he was considering her comfort was an odd concept to get her head around.

Replacing her artificial limbs with care, she made sure her advanced semi-robotic left hand operated as it should before padding silently to the bathroom. Checking her reflection in the mirror, she reached up to touch the wound on her neck and found it to be healed. Demons heal fast, she knew that much, and Daniel knew how to manipulate source energy for healing spells too. In the bathroom mirror, she examined the wound site. It was clean where Daniel had tended to it. It was about the only part of her that was.

A small scar had formed where the blade's tip had carved into her flesh. Had he been swifter to heal her, there might have been no scar at all, but looking at the ruined left side of her face where a piece of shrapnel had robbed her of what looks she'd once possessed, a new scar hardly mattered.

Setting the shower to run hot, she stripped off her final item of clothing and looked about for a bin into which she could throw them. That was when she spotted the shopping bags.

At whatever point Daniel had awoken, he hadn't simply crawled into bed. No, he had enough presence of mind to fetch supplies. One bag contained toiletries – all the things she could want. Even to the point that he'd bought tampons.

Lifting a shampoo bottle from the bag, Anastasia prised off the top to sniff in the scents contained within. For weeks she had been living like a homeless person. Why hadn't it occurred to her to have Benjamin open a portal into a hotel room somewhere. There were always empty suites, right?

Checking the next bag, she found clothes. Well, underwear at least. Suspecting there would be more elsewhere, she took the thick cotton robe from the back of the door and peered outside. Daniel was still asleep.

Tiptoeing through the hotel room, she found yet more bags, but the clothing she found was instantly pushed to one side when she found the bag containing food.

Okay, so it was pre-packed sandwiches, Coke, fruit, and chocolate bars, but she was hungry. Running back to the bathroom, she slumped to the cool tile with her back pressed against the door.

For all Daniel's faults, allowing for the fact that he tricked her and kidnapped her and even hurt her when they first met, she was prepared to forgive him. It wasn't as if they were lovers, or he was a boyfriend with expected standards of behaviour. He was a demon, and treachery went hand in hand with his nature.

Devouring a thick chicken and stuffing sandwich, a question popped into Anastasia's head. Picking up the discarded packet, she noted the price was in pounds. She was still in England then.

Pushing off the tile, she dropped the robe to the floor and stepped into the shower. It had been running for nearly five minutes and the air in the bathroom had filled with steam. Ten minutes later, her hair shampooed half to death and her skin exfoliated with another of the wonderful products Daniel had thoughtfully bought ... or stolen, Ana considered. It wouldn't exactly be hard for him to collect what he wanted and exit through a portal.

Regardless, she felt a whole lot better. Clean, no longer exhausted, and with something in her belly, she thought about what she wanted to do.

She needed to call Alex. Her friend would be worrying after so many hours without hearing from her. Ana had chosen not to tell the library research assistant that she was planning a minor excursion to rescue a demon from the house of the most powerful demon in existence. Alex would worry about the length of time since their last call, nevertheless.

More than alleviating her friend's concerns, Anastasia wanted to get back on with the task of tracking down the final pieces of armour. Some had been easy to locate, others less so, and with each piece Alex found, so the clues to the whereabouts of the remaining pieces dwindled.

Anastasia had accepted that she wasn't going to get it all. Pieces were lost, but she also told herself it didn't matter. She had enough already, and Jomana had proven that a few hours ago when the armour deflected the blow she tried to land.

The shield though, that was the piece Anastasia wanted. That and the helmet, another piece that was proving elusive. Alex had determined where the shield had been hidden, but it wasn't there when the four horsemen took her to collect it. Someone had beaten her to it and that gave birth to a lot of questions.

Was there someone else like her out there? A mortal who could touch the armour and the weapons without instantly dying. She'd been forced to watch when the verger in Rochester Cathedral grasped the sword and paid for it with his life. His scream echoed in her head again at the memory.

The shield had been hidden inside a cathedral in Mostar, a city in Croatia, so it could not have been a demon who took it, they could not step foot inside holy ground without their power draining away. According to Daniel, sustained time inside a church might kill a demon. Oddly the same was true for angels because of course earth's religions were all based on a lie, a false memory from too long ago in the past for anyone to know different.

Angels and demons were exactly the same race, only their ideals and beliefs separated them.

So who was it? Who took the shield? Who had it now? She would make it Alex's primary task to find out, and help her if she could, but right now, as a yawn split her face, she was going to get another couple of hours sleep.

Chapter 10

Reclining on the bed in his pokey, cheap hotel room, Zac stared at the ceiling. Tonight was not the first time he had tried to help, only to have his efforts thrown back at him. It made him question if he ought to accept his limitations and walk into the sunset. Nothing he did now or in the future would bring Gitta back and though he was fuelled by a desire to find Rebecca, Zac knew tearing her to shreds would do nothing to fill the void in his heart.

He couldn't be everywhere, and the one place he had chosen to be – here in Rome – had brought him nothing but rejection and frustration. In the morning, he would visit the pack again. Maybe they would listen once they'd been given time to think about things. If they did or if they didn't, he would move on.

Protecting shifters wasn't a mission he'd been given, or even one he intended to take on. Like so many things in life, it just happened that way. He started out trying to find others like him because he felt isolated. He was dangerous for humans to be around and for years he had kept to small communities and lived on the fringes. Recently though, as more and more people were discovering the magic inside themselves, as more and more shifters were being 'born', he was the one making contact with them.

He could be part of a community for the first time in his life, but it wasn't a leadership role he sought, it was company.

Eventually, sleep took him, his eyes growing heavy and closing without any conscious effort on his part.

Sleep did not last long.

The urgent hammering on his door ripped him from a dream about a tall blonde woman and a bucket of fish, and in his semi-panicked, barely-awake state, he was mid-way through transforming before he brought himself back under control.

"Zac! Zac! Are you in there?" the voice outside repeated a question it had already asked three times. Then it added, "We were attacked! They took my parents and at least two dozen others!"

Someone unseen snapped, "Break it down!"

The sound of a shoulder colliding with the door followed and then a hissed, yet urgent argument in the corridor outside his room.

There were several men – Zac was yet to hear a woman's voice – and the speaker who addressed him first was none other than Rocco Sifredi, the kid he'd rescued earlier.

"Never let a boy do a man's job," grumbled the same voice that wanted the door broken down.

"That's a bad idea, Carlo," Rocco argued.

"Get out of the way!" snapped a gruff voice – Zac assumed it was Carlo - as someone older and more determined shoved Rocco to one side. "This is how you break down a door."

Zac gripped the handle, counted in his head, and ripped the door open at precisely the right moment to make a fool of the man outside.

Standing behind the door to watch with a smirk on his face, Zac heard the yelp of surprise when Carlo's shoulder connected with free air. Unable to arrest his forward momentum, he stumbled, did his best to avoid the bed barely more than a metre beyond the door, and careened off it, smacking his shins on the steel frame with an audible clang.

Ignoring Carlo, Zac peered around the door to raise an eyebrow at his late-night visitors. Rumblings of complaint were coming from other rooms, arguments between men and women as one sought to deal with the noise and the other argued against escalating the situation.

Zac jerked his head. "Best you come inside before we have company."

There were four of them: Rocco, Carlo, and two Zac thought he might have seen in the bar earlier but couldn't be sure. They were TJ and Joshua. With the exception of Rocco, the other three were in their early thirties.

"So, the demons came again," he said it as a statement, his eyes on Rocco when he spoke.

"No! It wasn't demons! It was humans! It was the SIA! They raided us less than half an hour after you left the bar."

"I reckon they were looking for you," growled Carlo, falling silent when Zac gave him a warning look that required no translation.

Turning his attention back to Rocco and the other two, Zac asked, "How many?"

The pack members exchanged glances before Rocco said, "Maybe a hundred."

"It wasn't that many," argued Carlo instantly.

"It sure felt like it," countered TJ. "They were everywhere. A coordinated assault."

Rocco spoke over the top of the older men, "They were led by wizards, they used magic to subdue us."

"And to corral those who tried to escape," added TJ. "I ran into what felt like a brick wall and it was just air."

Narrowing his eyes, Zac asked, "Was there a German among them? Did you see a man in his early forties with a shaved head? Kinda ugly and wears a lot of black?"

Again they fired questioning looks at each other before agreeing that no one had seen anyone that matched that description.

Zac had been wondering if his old ... colleague, Zac wasn't sure how to refer to Otto Schneider, might be involved. They were not friends, but they were not enemies either. If he saw the German wizard again, he would approach him with a friendly, yet cautious demeanour. The wizard had his own agenda and Zac wasn't sure what it might be. It didn't align with his for sure.

The news said they were recruiting and training supernaturals. Could Otto be involved in that? Zac had no idea, but given the German's general attitude toward protecting the underdog – one thing the two of them had in common, he would not be surprised if the wizard was at the helm or close to it.

Dismissing the notion as irrelevant, Zac already knew what he was going to ask next.

"Where did they take them?"

Chapter 11

In a raid that became a melee - the target decided by the glut of reports from hundreds of witnesses to a werewolf fighting a giant man in the street - more than half of those rounded up were able to hold onto their phones. It was an oversight on the part of the local SIA who were afforded too little time to prepare for the raid and were too inexperienced to be sent on such a mammoth task.

Due to those facts, Rocco knew precisely where his parents had been taken. He wanted to get them back and that necessitated the visit to Zachary's hotel.

More than eighty percent of their pack had been captured in a single raid conducted by the SIA. It came without warning and could have any one of a dozen reasons behind it. The prevailing theory was they were seen as a threat to the local human community and were to be removed lest their presence attracted demons.

In truth, it was the SIA local commander enacting Ironbolt's latest policy. They were to forcibly recruit, that was the order. It played into

Director Roberto Alpi's hands - he saw a chance to remove a blight from the streets of Rome and chose to seize it.

There had been no reported demon incursions six months ago and when they started, they were so sporadic he could easily ignore them or write them off as likely false or fake. Now, though, it was every other night or worse and people were being reported as missing.

Whether they were human or otherwise, they were citizens of Rome, and he could protect everyone by gathering the supernaturals together. They would be interrogated and offered to Ironbolt for training. Whether that was in America, or – Alpi hoped – at a new camp he would create, did not yet matter.

Reports of werewolves fighting in the open, terrifying citizens with their display, felt serendipitous. He could justify every one of his actions should he need to. He was just obeying orders after all.

Now, an hour after the raid, those who had been collected were in holding beneath his building. It wasn't just the werewolves – who were kind enough to all gather in one place to make collecting them easy – Alpi's teams had gathered a further twenty-seven known or suspected witches and wizards from across the city. Some of them had come peacefully, others less so, but his forces included a powerful elemental magician – a former demon familiar whose abilities far exceeded anyone who had developed their power on earth.

Those taken tonight were all secured downstairs now, where his advisers assured him, they were cut off from the ley lines. The shifters could still transform, but there would be no magic from the wizards until Alpi said so.

What Alpi did not know, was the small force of shifters on their way to his facility and the giant, immortal werewolf leading them.

Chapter 12

Pummelled into unconsciousness, Benjamin awoke to find himself no longer in the dungeon deep beneath Beelzebub's palace. He was surrounded by demons, all of whom he knew by name. None of them were talking and all wore unfriendly grimaces.

He was on the floor; plush carpet beneath his hands as he pushed himself upright into a kneeling position. No one moved to stop him, and the silence continued until a familiar voice boomed from across the room.

"Leave us."

Benjamin twisted his head, spotting Beelzebub above the heads of the demons as they filed silently from the room to leave him alone with their master.

Beelzebub had his back to the angel, paying him little attention as he poured himself a drink. There was nothing to stop Benjamin from opening a portal and escaping. He could be gone before Beelzebub had a chance to stop him.

"Drink?"

The question caught Benjamin by surprise. Seeing no reason to stay on his knees and berating himself for questioning if he ought to rise, he got to his feet.

The lord of the demons turned to face him with a crystal tumbler in each hand.

"Bourbon?" he offered Benjamin a glass and took a sip of the other. "You're probably wondering why you are not currently locked in the rooms beneath this house."

Benjamin took the offered drink without taking his eyes from Beelzebub.

"What are your intentions?" he asked.

Walking away again, his glass held to his mouth as he drank more of the dark liquid, Beelzebub crossed the room to a door.

Pausing before he opened it, Beelzebub looked back at Benjamin with an expression the angel couldn't read.

In the moment when he realised he wasn't going to be able to escape, Benjamin had tried to open a portal, only to be denied the chance as he was swarmed by demons. Fleetingly, just before he lost consciousness, he acknowledged the misery his life was about to become.

That he hadn't awoken to find himself strapped inside a vile machine of torture was throwing him.

"Mostly," Beelzebub said, "I would like you to relax." He opened the door and stepped out of the way as unseen figures on the other side came forward.

"Megwin?" Benjamin blurted, shocked to see the female angel coming into the room. His disbelieving eyes almost sprang from his head when another angel he knew followed her and then two more appeared.

Megwin came to him. "It's so good to see you again," she kissed his cheeks and stood aside to let the others greet him.

Beelzebub interrupted before Benjamin could ask any of the many questions in his head.

"Your friends are here because they no longer wish to follow my brother. I believe, Benjamin, that you are of the same opinion. There is a place here for you. I have no desire for the opposing factions of our ancient race to kill each other. Too many precious lives have already been lost."

Megwin reached out to take Benjamin's hand.

"Stay with us, Benjamin. Help us to make the transition of rule as beneficial as it can be. Godfrey cannot win; we all know that, so help us to preserve humankind under Beelzebub's reign."

Benjamin looked from Megwin to the others and then to Beelzebub himself.

Choosing his words carefully, he said, "There are more angels we can recruit."

Chapter 13

Waking again, this time with a start, Anastasia's heart caught in her chest. It pounded like a drum, only to subside a moment later when her memory filled in the blanks.

Levering herself off the mattress, she squinted at the clock. It was just after midnight.

Daniel had woken her, the demon shifting in his sleep to rub against her arm. The unfamiliar sensation of a live being against her skin in bed and at night had caused her to rouse in a panicked state, but now, looking down at Daniel's slumbering form, she considered her options.

How long had it been for her? Too long that was for sure. How likely was she to die in the coming days, weeks, or months?

She couldn't do the math on that one either, but the likelihood was high.

Reaching an easy decision, she slid the covers away from Daniel's body. He was naked. With a hand that threatened to tremble, she placed her palm on the soft skin of his abdomen. Feeling the taut muscle beneath and revelling in it, she kept her hand there and lowered her torso, nuzzling into the warmth of his neck and leaving gentle kisses in a trail as she moved her lips toward his.

"Are you sure this is what you want?"

When he spoke without Ana even realising he was awake, her whole body tensed and she almost recoiled. Though she flinched, she didn't move away.

To answer his question, she sat up in the bed, pulled the plain white t-shirt she wore up and over her head, and straddled him. With her lips on his, everything else came easily. She had not had sex since before the accident that tore off two of her limbs. Because of her brain injury she couldn't remember anything before that, so though she knew she was not a virgin, she had no memory of ever having had sex before.

Their movements were frantic and urgent, the answer to a question that had never been asked. That they were drawn to each other through their mutual circumstance did not need to be explored, all they needed in that moment was the gift each had for the other.

All too soon, it was over, and the reality that they had to move on before the sun rose was upon them.

"You know," Daniel said, his voice husky and filled with hunger as he watched Ana heading toward the bathroom, her derriere swaying enticingly, "We have at least forty minutes until the sun comes up."

They filled the time they had without the need for words, and it was only when Anastasia explored the clothes Daniel had for her that she spoke again.

"Did you get me a hoody?"

Already dressed in a fitted shirt, jacket, and trousers, the demon raised an eyebrow.

Ana groaned. "I need a hoody to hide my face. Facial recognition stuff is everywhere now, and my ugly mug is being shown everywhere around the world. Getting recognised will do us no favours at all."

Daniel's tone was unconcerned when he replied, "We'll get you one when we arrive."

Strapping on the sheath for her sword, which rested at a slight angle down the centre of her back so the handle sat proud of her shoulders and was easy to draw, Ana asked, "Where are we going?"

"America. Louisiana to be exact. There's a place there that serves the best gumbo and that's what I'm in the mood for."

Anastasia's stomach growled, reminding her how little she'd eaten in the last day.

The sun was beginning to tinge the skyline and the time to be elsewhere was overdue. They travelled with the darkness, stepping through a portal to arrive at night on the other side of the Atlantic where the sun had only just set.

Sending Daniel to find her a hooded garment, Anastasia cursed at herself for making Alex wait so long. She'd meant to call her last night, but fell asleep. Then planned to call her when she awoke, but found herself engaged in … other activities.

Ducking into an alcove so she was out of sight, Ana turned on the burner phone Daniel obtained at the same time as everything else. He hadn't paid for any of it, but then what is money to a demon from an alternate realm?

"Hello?" Alex's voice answered tentatively.

"It's Ana," Anastasia said, breathing a sigh of relief to hear her friend's voice. She had no reason to suspect the demons could find Alex, but that didn't mean she didn't worry. They would kill her in a heartbeat.

Alex wasted no time in going full mother mode. "Ana, where the hell have you been?"

With a snort of amusement, Ana said, "Hell. That's where I've been. Benjamin and I went to rescue Daniel last night."

There was stunned silence from the other end.

To fill it, Anastasia added, "I got him. He's in one piece."

In her tiny apartment just outside Pisa in Italy, Alex's frown had driven her eyebrows together to form one large, long hairy caterpillar.

"Why, Ana? Why would you risk everything to rescue that scumbag demon?"

"She's on speakerphone," Daniel announced, arriving next to Anastasia clutching a black hoody in his right hand.

Unabashed, Alex raised her voice. "You're a scumbag, Daniel. I wouldn't spit on you if you were on fire. He's going to betray you the first chance he gets, Ana. He's done it before. I don't care how pretty he is, he cannot be trusted."

Anastasia, frowning just as hard as her friend, argued, "He's not that bad. I think he's turned over a new leaf. When I got him out, he ... well, he's been thinking about my needs, not just his own."

A beat of silence followed before Alex jumped to a conclusion Anastasia would rather they didn't discuss.

"Oh, my God! You had sex with him!"

Shushing into the phone while Daniel chortled to himself, Ana said, "Will you keep it down." She wanted to deny it, but lying to a friend wasn't in her nature. "It ... it was a spur of the moment thing, okay? It had been a long time for me, and I keep thinking I am about to die."

Alex shot back, "It's been a long time for me too, babe, and with your body you can do better than a demon. Yes, yes, I know you have a scar on your face, and you think men will be put off when they discover your stumps, but having a bottom the size of Bournemouth puts them off faster, I can tell you."

Somehow they had vanished down a rabbit hole of whose sex life was the most miserable, so in a bid to steer things back on track, Ana admitted the key piece of information she had until then left out.

"I lost Benjamin. I couldn't get them both out. The demons came and there was no way to get to him."

"Really, Ana? You rescued the scumbag demon and left behind the wonderful and sweet-natured angel."

"Again," Daniel remarked. "Still on speakerphone. Anyway, I'm a top-drawer shag. So, if you're in need of …"

Ana shut him off with a hard kick to the shins.

"Really, Daniel? We were still at it half an hour ago and now you're hitting on my friend."

Daniel moved out of range, smiling when he offered a broad shrug. "Hey, I'm a demon. What were you expecting? A ring?"

"You see?" exclaimed Alex. "Scumbag demon and you let him …"

Ana cut her off mid-sentence. "All right, all right. It won't happen again." She mostly meant it. Somehow they had circled back to sex. Moving the conversation on, Anastasia raised another key piece of news. "I got the sword."

"The sword? You got the sword?"

Ana nodded even though Alex couldn't see it.

"I did. Beelzebub will come after it though. I need you to find the shield, Alex."

"Ah, well, I've been thinking about that one myself."

Anastasia's ears pricked up hoping to hear good news.

"It's not good news, I'm afraid."

Anastasia cursed.

"I think you need to go back to Mostar, babes. Someone there must know who ended up with it. We were in and out so fast last time we never got a chance to do any detective work and honestly, I'm struggling to find worthwhile leads for the remaining pieces. Going after the shield is your next best bet anyway."

Accepting the news for what it was, Anastasia ended the call with a promise to stay in touch.

Seeing Ana end the call, Daniel checked the time.

"It's still dark there. We'll travel once we've eaten."

Chapter 14

"It's a ninety-four percent positive hit, Sir."

Colt Ironbolt, president of the SIA had been waiting for this news for too long already. People expected results. His nation expected results, and even though the world in general knew little of Anastasia Aaronson, she had been listed as an international terrorist and her photo was everywhere. When she was apprehended by his people – Ironbolt congratulated himself for not mentally labelling them as 'men', being politically correct if he planned to run for the ultimat e office was important – he would make sure it was his name associated with her arrest.

Sophisticated facial recognition software from across the civilised world was ready to find her the moment she walked in front of a camera. That had occurred just twice in recent weeks and on those two occasions she was long gone before anyone could deploy.

Familiars though, that was the key. Otto Schneider's rescued familiars were able to open a portal between the realms, a neat trick the German wizard had taught them that involved wearing a glove made from the skin of one of those disgusting, sexless shilt creatures.

It took a level of ability beyond many of the younger wizards who had recently found magic awakening within them, but the older ones took to it easily. Ironbolt knew this not because Schneider willingly revealed his secrets – the German was frustratingly tight-lipped and refused to acknowledge rank or hierarchy, but through a simple trick of asking someone else.

There were so many familiars; Ironbolt found one who needed something and leveraged a spy within Schneider's operation.

"Sir?" Ayla Pendragon, Ironbolt's right hand ... almost slipped up ... woman, was waiting for a response.

"Send teams. Send all the teams if you have to. Anastasia Aaronson has a weapon that we need. They need to bring her in alive if at all possible."

"What if she is still travelling with a demon, Sir?"

Ironbolt gave a small shake of his head that no one else saw. "Tell our agents to not bother coming back if they get killed," he spat flippantly. "We need that weapon."

His mind was already thinking through what he would say to the press.

Six floors below Ironbolt's office, Ayla Pendragon kept her thoughts on the boss to herself.

"Deploy six teams. All supers. No humans. I want a familiar in each pair and ..." She debated her decision for enough seconds that her immediate subordinate pressed her to finish what she was saying.

"Ma'am?"

Gritting her teeth in a grimace, Ayla committed to what she knew was the right decision.

"Send Katja Weber."

Luther Kranti's eyes flared at the inclusion of the fifteen-year-old girl, but he knew why Mrs Pendragon wanted her included. The girl could control and repel hellfire. Her inclusion on the mission might be the difference between winning and losing, living and dying.

Regardless of that, as Luther passed on the commands, he knew Otto Schneider was going to go nuts.

What he didn't know, was that the order to deploy and who they were going up against was received by someone outside of the organisation. Someone who would act upon it.

Chapter 15

Feeling a little bloated from all the food she'd just forced into her stomach, Anastasia slumped back in her chair. Under different circumstances, the setting would be called romantic. She was sitting opposite a man ... well, okay, a demon, but he looked like a man on the surface – who she had recently had sex with. It had been good too.

To her left, his right, was a lake, the lights of the restaurant reflected on the water where the ever-moving surface made them dance and play.

She felt like reaching across the table to hold his hand. For others it could be a perfect moment, but for Anastasia it was just a lie, and she knew it. There was no love between her and Daniel, yet at the same time he was the closest she had come to having a boyfriend in two years. It was a crappy statistic for a twenty-three-year-old.

Her life was a mess, though not through choice and she assigned herself no blame for arriving at this point. None of it was down to her.

Her line of thought caused her to ask, "What am I?"

Daniel had been looking across the water, his thoughts his own though Anastasia worried he might be wallowing in the memory of his recent incarceration and torture. At the sound of her voice, he turned to face her, an open expression displaying almost no emotion.

"I mean," Ana continued. "I'm not a wizard; I cannot perform elemental magic like Otto Schneider. And I'm not a shifter, but obviously I'm not an angel or a demon either." She left the question hanging, her words a tempting hook for him to bite.

Daniel exhaled and looked down at his hands where they rested in his lap. When he looked back up, Anastasia was expecting a big revelation – she thought he was taking his time so he could try to figure out what to tell her, but his answer was to be a disappointment.

"I don't know. As you say, you are none of the things I can identify." He looked out over the bay again. "My best guess is that somewhere in your distant lineage is a demon or an angel. You already know all those under eighteen years of age were left behind by the death curse, trapped here in the mortal realm to live out their expected lifespan among humanity."

"What became of the children?" Ana pressed. "Does anyone know?"

She got a shrug in response. "There is no way to know. However, since the world as you know it is not dominated and ruled over by a magical race of beings, I think it safe to assume the small number that were left behind were assimilated into the human population. Some worried that the humans, when they awoke one day to find the hierarchy of the ruling race was completely gone, might have turned on the children who were left, overpowering and slaughtering them. Others take that a stage further to hypothesise that the elder children would have fought back and escaped with their younger siblings."

"That's why mortals are finding magic awakening inside their bodies right now, isn't it?"

Still looking out at the dark waves, Daniel nodded slowly. "Yes. It stands to reason that the children survived and over time, they bred with the humans. I don't know if they hid their magic, fearing for how it might be received, or if the death curse disabled their ability to summon it. Whichever it was, over time the remainder of my race left in the mortal realm were watered down to nothing."

"Until now."

"Well," Daniel allowed a wry smile to crease his face. "Until a few hundred years ago when the shilt began to find their way back here. That was when I started to look for familiars and discovered magic still existed here. It was weak, but as the death curse's power dwindled, so the magic grew stronger, manifesting in mortals at an ever-increasing rate."

"But you can't guess what makes me so different to everyone else?" Ana circled back to her original question.

The truth was that Daniel had a fairly good idea as to what Anastasia was and genuinely hoped he was wrong. Either way, it wasn't something he was ready to share yet.

Disappointed that he had nothing useful to tell her, but not surprised, Anastasia pulled the hoody back up around her head.

"I suppose we are just going to open a portal and vanish without paying for our food then?"

Daniel pulled a mockingly innocent face – whatever could she possibly mean? As Ana hiked an accusing eyebrow, the demon reached inside his jacket and from it produced a wallet.

Unable to hide her disbelief, Ana asked, "Where did you get that? I thought you stole all the toiletries and clothes at the last place."

Frowning as he laid a credit card on the table, Daniel sniggered, "I did. I stole this too. It was hanging out of a back pocket."

Anastasia's jaw hung open. As a British Army officer, integrity had been a big part of her code. Okay, so now she was a fugitive from the law around the planet even though all she was trying to do was help, but stealing things and taking what she needed from others, such as dinner tonight, did not sit right with her.

The waitress came by, producing a card reader onto which Daniel tapped the card. With receipt in hand, he pushed back his chair and in an unexpected chivalrous act, went around the table to assist Anastasia with her chair.

"You're making me worry," she hissed at him. "Stop being nice. Just because we had sex, don't go getting all weird with me."

If he had a glib comment, she never got to hear it because the front wall of the restaurant chose that moment to explode.

Chapter 16

A blast of inrushing air, as unstoppable as a tsunami wave, swept through the restaurant clearing everything in its path. Tables, chairs, couples eating their evening meal and the wait staff hustling here and there, were powerless to resist the energy contained within the blast wave.

Oddly, the restaurant's front wall had exploded outward, vanishing into the night sky in the millisecond before the storm of air hit. Anastasia and Daniel both knew why the two things failed to correlate.

The air was conjured.

In the half heartbeat before the wall exploded outward, and the shockwave smashed into her, Anastasia saw who was behind it.

The horsemen were here. How they had found her she could not guess, and she knew the next few seconds were too precious to be wasted on futile questions.

Letting the irresistible force of the air carry her backward out of the building, she tumbled over the edge and fell. Expecting to find water beneath her, the air was driven from her lungs when she discovered a concrete path running along the water's edge.

"Daniel! We need a portal!" she blurted between painful gasps of air.

With no time to lose, she conjured the remaining charge of hellfire spindled inside her body and withdrew the sword from a sheath on her back. With a grunt of effort against the pain reporting in from several sources, she tensed her leg muscles. She was going to grab Daniel and escape with him. It didn't matter where they went, just so long as they put some distance between them and the horsemen.

The wall above her head exploded, showering Anastasia in pieces of brick and splinters of wood. From inside the restaurant came cries of pain and screams of terror that were shut off so abruptly Ana knew the horsemen were killing people in their bid to get to her.

"Daniel," she snapped her head up to make sure he was there and caught a split-second glimpse of his panicked face as a portal closed with him on the other side.

"Daniel!"

He had left her. The stinking rat had left her. In her heart she knew why: he had been captured and tortured and the horsemen were here for him almost as much as they were for her. Even if they couldn't get her, taking Daniel back so Beelzebub could continue his torment would curry them favour.

Since his rescue, he'd acted as if nothing had happened and that his weeks of torture had little to no effect on him. Yet here was the evidence. The first sign of trouble and he ran.

Rising from the concrete and stepping over the ruined remains of the backwall, Anastasia accepted her position for what it was. There was nowhere for her to run to and why should she? They couldn't kill her … at least, they were probably expected to bring her back alive, but even if Beelzebub had permitted a kill order, she was wearing a suit of magical armour, possessed not one but two weapons she could use to permanently end an immortal demon, and she'd already killed their fourth member, Martha.

A bolt of hellfire, aimed at a petrified waitress too scared to seek refuge, sizzled into Ana's skin when she blocked its path with her right arm.

Aksel, the demon who threw it, drew back his teeth in a leer. In his left hand was another orb of hellfire, glowing a murky dark red. In his right was a long sword, easily twice the length of Anastasia's. Along its length, signals seemed to glow from within.

Anastasia narrowed her eyes, challenging the powerful demon without the need to speak.

Bitrius appeared across the restaurant to her left, his arrival sparking her into motion. Anastasia ran, leaping through the broken back wall to land once more on the concrete outside. Feet pumping, she gained distance, cutting left to get away from the water and then climbing when she found a fire escape.

She needed to get the fight away from innocent people. Loose orbs of hellfire, flung her way only to miss, would continue onward until they hit something. In Osaka, the destruction wrought by a battle started by Daniel and then made worse by the arrival of Benjamin, had claimed several lives. Ana didn't know how many because she made a point of avoiding the news. If anything, this area was even more densely populated than the Japanese city, and she needed to do what she could to reduce the loss of life.

Climbing the external staircase, her feet rapping on the steel like a drum being played, it started to rain.

"Perfect," she mumbled to herself. As a soldier rain had been her friend: it deadened the sound she and the soldiers under her command made, allowing them to move more stealthily. Here though, all it did was get her wet. She knew the demons would call up their second sight and be able to spot her wherever she went – hiding when you have a magical aura is a futile exercise.

Stepping off the ladder three stories up to find herself on a flat roof, Anastasia walked to the centre and waited.

She didn't have to wait long.

Acadus was the first to arrive, propelling himself up and over the side of the roof using elemental magic to conjure a cushion of air. Ana had seen them perform the trick before, her jealousy at the power of flight held in check only by the belief she would probably crash and die if she tried it.

Not that she could.

Bitrius and Aksel arrived moments later, the three demons spread out to draw her focus – she couldn't watch all of them at once.

Creating a triangle with Anastasia at the centre, the demons were each more than twenty metres away from their target.

"One chance," Bitrius raised his voice to be heard above the beating rain. "You come with us, or we destroy this town as we try to take you."

Anastasia, the rain running over her face and dripping off her chin, had already pushed back her hoody to stop it interfering with her peripheral vision.

To answer Bitrius, she drew source energy from the core of her body, channelling it from the earth to fuel her magic. Forming a light blue orb of sinfire in her hand – her hellfire was exhausted already - she watched, checking over her shoulders to see who would move first.

They were wary, but they were also here because they believed they could beat her. Beelzebub wanted the sword back, and he wanted the suit of armour. They had failed him already, allowing the tiny slip of a mortal woman to escape when she killed Martha in Egypt.

They could not afford to fail a second time.

Shock registered in Ana's eyes when she saw Acadus form hellfire. There was no good reason to use it - not only could it not kill her as it did other mortals, it made her stronger. He fired the orbs, but not at her, they went wide and by then it was already late for her to see the diversion tactic for what it was.

Bitrius and Aksel were running at her, Acadus charging too now and forming fresh hellfire. Sure, hitting her with it would fire her up, but enough of it could stop Ana in her tracks and that might be all the advantage they would need.

Spinning, and driving off hard to get from stationary to sprint, Anastasia aimed for Acadus, the least prepared of the three. Switching from left hand to right, she pushed sinfire into the God Sword. From the corner of her eye, she saw the obsidian blade light up from within.

She leapt, swinging the deadly weapon to make the demon duck back. The blade missed its target, but Anastasia had never expected to be able to draw so easy a strike. Coming down to the hard roof of the building, she gritted her teeth against the impending impact and folded her legs.

Acadus swept the sword from his back, swinging down to chop through the air where he expected her head to be.

Landing painfully on her knees and shins, Ana slid across the slick surface now covered in several millimetres of rainwater. Converting her slide, she whipped the sword around tagging Acadus on his right calf to open a wound that felled him.

Still sliding on her knees, Ana used her left hand to grab the ground and spin herself, coming up into a crouch as the other two horsemen arrived next to their colleague. She risked a smile in their direction, her chestnut hair falling across her face to hide the scar until she flicked it out of the way.

"Feeling nervous, boys?"

In reply to her question, the fallen horseman got back up, his wound refusing to heal because the God Sword made it. This was likely the first time he had bled in over four thousand years. To Anastasia it was the most annoying thing about the demons: their immortality. No matter what she did, they came back unharmed. Until she got her hands on the sword that is.

Doing what she hoped they would not expect, Ana threw out her left hand, a sustained stream of sinfire hitting Bitrius in the chest when she altered her trajectory at the last moment to catch him unprepared. Not that preparation would have done much to change what happened.

The raw energy contained within picked the demon from the rooftop like so much detritus, tossing him in a jumbled mess of limbs toward the edge of the roof. He might have gone over had Aksel not thrown a short dagger at Anastasia's face.

The suit of armour protected her body where it covered, but it wasn't a complete suit and the exposed parts, such as her head, were vulnerable.

The flying object missed, though not by much, and swiftly proved to be just another diversionary tactic as Acadus, running at her despite his pronounced limp, swept upward with his sword.

She darted backward to get away, and when she started to correct the move, Aksel hit her with hellfire. The first blast was a surprise she didn't see coming. It made her ears ring where it found its aiming mark on the crown of her skull. She absorbed it, thankful for the extra juice, and was ready for the next one.

Or so she thought.

Coordinated, whether by accident or design, all three horsemen hit her with hellfire. The barrage, all coming at once created enough of a shockwave to drive her back another yard.

And that took her over the edge of the roof.

Chapter 17

It was not the first time Katja had travelled by portal, but that did not mean she was used to it. Doing her best to act like it was no big deal, the fifteen-year-old witch felt her stomach tighten in the moment before she stepped through.

"Really? That's what you're wearing to battle the most dangerous person on the planet?"

The question came from Wanda, Katja's partner for the trip, and was delivered with a snarky, sarcastic tone.

Glancing down at her clothes, Katja said, "What's wrong with them?" They said to hurry and with it being early evening, she had been dressed in her usual clothes: designer sweatpants, a matched stretchy, low-cut top that exposed just a little cleavage – she had spotted Tommy Hobbs the moment she arrived – and a denim jacket exactly like the one Bethany Cooper was wearing in the video for her latest chart-topping song.

Wanda grunted something Katja didn't catch and left her behind as she headed for the briefing room.

The team had been given only minutes to get ready; time was of the essence very clearly. Paired with Wanda, one of the familiars who escaped from the immortal realm with Otto, Katja wanted to ask a whole bunch of questions: What was it like with the demons? How are you adjusting to life here? When were you born and how old are you? Oh, and here's a big one – have you seen Otto Schneider and how do I get hold of him?

Her days since arriving in America were not what she had expected. Sure she got to eat American food and candy and watch American TV, but that was nowhere near as exciting as she imagined it would be. She joined a team of new supernaturals converging from around the world to be trained as a force that might defend humanity from the demon threat. Varying in age, nationality, and race, they weren't allowed out, and though they all knew they could break out easily enough if they chose to, they were being good.

For now.

She was yet to see Otto Schneider, the wizard who had rescued her so many times now and who lured her to America with the promise of safety and purpose – she was to be a major part of a force that would stop the demons when they came. There was no number by which she could contact him and all she knew was that he was out in the world somewhere trying to find more of the familiars – people he considered to be among the most powerful supernaturals in the mortal realm.

Of course, Katja was denied the chance to ask Wanda anything because they needed to haul ass.

Haul ass. The term brought a smirk to Katja's face. Americans had such great phrases. The smirk soon faded when she stepped out of the portal.

Six teams were all coming through in separate places clustered around the site where Anastasia Aaronson had been seen.

Katja knew of Anastasia only from the TV where she was talked about like she might be the most dangerous person on the planet, and from a few pieces of footage the twins had shown her. Cassie and Jennifer were here tonight too, and it gave Katja some comfort to have someone she knew along for the ride.

They were older than Katja by a couple of years and had taken the young German girl under their wings the day she arrived, that being their nature – they were good, charitable Christian girls.

Arriving in the streets of Slidell, Louisiana, Katja had enough time to realise it was raining and that she wasn't dressed for it before she felt the presence of magic. A burst of hellfire, lighting the night sky high above was reflected off the clouds above. It came from the rooftop of a building less than a hundred metres away.

Wanda, a short black woman with hair shaved down to her scalp, gripped the young girl's arm, and held her in place.

"Behind me," she ordered, taking charge. "That was hellfire."

"I know," Katja pushed the arm away. "I've seen it before."

If Wanda had a reply, it was cut off by a scream as someone fell from the building they were both looking at.

Katja's eyes locked on the figure as gravity gripped it, sucking it down. Without needing to think, she drew on the ley line she tapped the moment she stepped through the portal and conjured air. Manipulating it with her hands for fine control, she pushed out with her senses.

A bead of sweat forming on her brow went unnoticed among the raindrops and Katja held her breath to focus everything on catching the falling woman.

"That could be a demon!" Wanda warned, the flash of hellfire putting her on high alert.

"Or," Katja grunted as she funnelled her air spell to bring the person now caught on her cushion of air closer, "it could be the very person we were sent here to collect."

Was it going to be this simple? *'Go and get Anastasia Aaronson so she can do no more harm. We have a purpose-built cell in which we plan to contain her.'* Katja questioned if she was going to achieve precisely that within a minute of arriving and without walking more than five metres.

Wanda snatched at her radio, touching the send button.

"This is green team. I think we have her. Stand by for confirmation."

Anastasia wasn't sure who had caught her, and half expected to see Otto Schneider controlling the spell that prevented her from going splat on the pavement after a three-story drop. Would the armour have saved her? She seriously doubted it. More likely it would have kept all her bits in one easy-to-scoop-up mess.

Twisting her body around to see not only where she was going but to find the person manipulating the cloud of invisible air on which she was riding, Ana found she was heading for two women.

A moment later she corrected her assessment: One was a woman, but the other, the one controlling the spell, was a teenage girl. Her outfit gave away her age as much as anything.

A screaming orb of hellfire overtook Anastasia's magic cloud ride and by the time a second one shot by half a second later, the spell keeping her aloft fifteen feet above the ground had been abandoned. Yet again, Anastasia fell.

Wanda yelled in horror. "Demons!" It wasn't just the Aaronson woman; she had her pet demon with her or so she assumed from the appearance of hellfire. Like everyone else, Wanda had no idea how the arrangement worked or what the pair were trying to achieve, but it cleared away any doubt that the suspected supernatural terrorist was anything other than exactly what everyone said she was.

Darting to the side as she pulled up a defensive shield to protect herself, Wanda realised the girl she'd been partnered with hadn't moved.

There was no time to shout a warning, and the orbs of hellfire were coming straight for Katja where she stood too frightened to move.

Dropping the manipulation of air, Katja drew yet more elemental energy into her body. To her, as the hellfire flew toward her body, it was as if time stood still. Casually, she observed that Anastasia Aaronson was falling again. The distance was greater than she would have liked, but she also believed the woman would survive. Perhaps a few injuries would slow her down and make her easier to catch.

As her body filled to the point of overflow, Katja's feet lifted off the street on which she stood. She liked being airborne, it made her feel powerful and in control. More than that, she enjoyed how other supernaturals looked at her when she loaded up with so much magical energy it made her float.

Reaching out with her senses, just as she had in Bremen when she last faced a demon, she felt the hellfire – its essence and nature, the source energy that powered it.

In Bremen she had redirected the hellfire back at the demon who threw it, or harmlessly into the ground. Given weeks to think about how it worked, she chose to do something different.

She reduced it to atoms and discarded it on the wind.

Crouching behind her shield, Wanda couldn't believe her eyes.

A voice crackled over her radio, "Green team. What's happening? Wanda? Come in. Over."

Anastasia spotted her landing, which is to say she knew which bit of the earth she was going to hit and was able to work out which parts of her body she wanted to be most terribly bruised.

As she expected, the armour did nothing to cushion the fall which left her head ringing, and the taste of blood in her mouth. Levering herself from the surface of the street with actions as swift as she could make them – everything hurt and her limbs did not want to work – she glanced along the street to the teenage girl who was now floating three feet off the ground, and back up to the roof from which she had just fallen.

"Mental note," she paused to spit out a glob of blood-infused saliva, "don't go up on roofs."

The horsemen could have been right behind her, but they were not. Was that a good thing or bad?

More worried about them than the floating girl, Anastasia continued to watch the rooftops, a sinfire orb readied in her left hand and the God Sword powered up and ready until another tug of magical air lifted her from the ground once more.

"We have her," Wanda reported across the radio waves from behind her shield. "We have Anastasia Aaronson. The demon she travels with is here too though. Converge on my location, but stay sharp."

Anastasia was thankful for the assist when falling to her death, but she had no interest in whatever the girl wanted and was becoming annoyed by her interference. With her feet off the ground there was nothing she could do to arrest her forward motion, so she fired a bolt of sinfire in the teenage girl's direction, purely as a warning.

The girl's spell shut off, just as it had before, and Anastasia fell to the pavement. Mercifully, it was only a few feet beneath her this time, and she hit the ground running. In two paces and the blink of an eye, she was lost from sight behind a building.

Katja hadn't intended to let her go. It was the sinfire that caught her off guard. She'd never seen it before and flinched when it came screaming her way.

Cursing, Wanda reported the change in situation to the other teams, all of whom were hotfooting it to get to them. Running after their target and shouting for Katja to follow, Wanda's feet ground to a halt when a portal opened ten metres ahead of her.

Chapter 18

B lasting Anastasia from the rooftop, Bitrius had launched himself into the air to follow, but the arrival of new supernaturals and the injury to Acadus gave him pause.

A moment to regroup would not hurt and perhaps there were yet more prizes to be gained tonight. Supernatural mortals in the vicinity meant the chance to gather familiars – a peace offering to their lord who was yet to forgive them for failing to bring back the armour he coveted so deeply.

Expecting to see Anastasia Aaronson hit the ground and sustain injuries, the demons were disappointed to see one of the supernaturals 'catch' her. When she then performed the impossible, making Aksel's hellfire vanish in mid-air, they knew who they were looking at.

Beelzebub had talked about her, about the young girl who had been Teague's familiar for just a few hours before Otto Schneider turned up to rescue her. That she was somehow imbued with such power was unprecedented and confusing. However, that just made her even more cherished as a prize to take back with them.

Seeing Anastasia flee into a side street, the three horsemen split. Each opened a portal and stepped through.

Bitrius emerged in front of Katja Weber, Acadus behind, while Aksel dropped himself in front of Anastasia.

Wanda opened her mouth to shout a warning to her young charge. Raising her shield to protect her front, she was hit from behind by hellfire.

Acadus had thrown it, doing so as he opened the portal and before he'd even stepped through it. There was nothing Katja could do to stop it from killing her partner, there just wasn't enough time.

With demons either side of her, she was conjuring a fresh barrage of spells when Wanda's lifeless body crumpled to the ground.

Beyond Bitrius, Katja could see at least two more teams coming her way. One was airborne, using their skills to cover the ground faster, but neither was going to be in time to help her.

Acadus, knowing he couldn't employ hellfire, had chosen a simple manipulation of air. It cut off the oxygen reaching Katja's lungs, terrifying the teenager when she tried to breathe and couldn't. That wasn't enough though. The demon's plan was to use her to make Anastasia surrender.

Anastasia's ability to wield source energy might be unexplainable, but all three of the remaining horsemen had witnessed the mortal woman's unwillingness to let another human die. The British woman had fought tooth and nail to protect her friend when they held them both captive. She would do the same for this girl and if she paused to rethink her tactics, they would take them both.

Waiting at the far end of the side street to head Anastasia off and hold her until Bitrius and Acadus had the girl, Aksel was starting to wonder if he might have missed something. Aaronson ought to be in sight by now. He could see the other end of the back street for that matter.

Advancing slowly, for she had to be hiding in the shadows, he saw when she stepped out from a doorway and flashed him a smile.

"You never did come across as particularly bright, Aksel," Ana remarked with humour in her tone. "What are you going to do now?"

Tightening the grip on his sword, Aksel flicked his eyes past the mortal to the street beyond. Acadus and Bitrius ought to be appearing any second. They were to grab the German girl as a prize for Beelzebub and help him to corner Anastasia. The three of them could return to the demon realm victorious, taking their lord and master gifts that would reinstate them in his eyes.

But where were they? Fear was a new emotion for the demons, immortality making them complacent. But were they immortal? Aksel watched when the diminutive female human had killed Martha in Egypt. The mortal ended Martha's life, and she wasn't the first. Every demon in the immortal realm saw when Anastasia killed Nathaniel, one of Beelzebub's generals.

Aksel's gaze shifted again, twitching to lock on Anastasia when she swished the God Sword and began to advance.

His right foot almost took a step back, the muscles in his leg tensing before he corrected the motion and drew source energy into his body instead. Hellfire couldn't kill Anastasia, but it would distract and slow her down. He was facing her alone and she had already hurt him once this evening.

Anastasia's smile widened. One on one with Aksel? She liked her odds.

Fifty metres from her location, Katja's eyes were starting to bug from her head. She couldn't breathe and panic had set in. She knew it was nothing more than a manipulation of an air spell – one she'd learned at the academy, but calming her mind so she could fight it was proving difficult. Her partner, an older and vastly more experienced witch was lying dead at her feet, and she was pinned between two demons whose calm, almost nonchalant demeanour was unnerving.

Dancing lights appeared in the corners of Katja's vision to drive a fresh spike of fear through her. One of the demons grabbed her right arm, steering her down the street though she could barely feel his grip on her flesh past the pounding in her head.

The other SIA teams were arriving, but both demons were throwing hellfire at them, keeping them pinned down for fear of instant death and the humans were doing nothing. Initially confused by the lack of attack, Katja's fog-filled brain took several seconds to figure out her colleagues were holding back for fear of hurting her.

Her eyes found Cassie's, the young American girl risking a peek from around the building she hid behind. Then she was gone again, darting back into cover, half a second before the wall by her head exploded, when hellfire struck it.

No one was coming to save her, and the two demons were steering Katja toward a side street – the same one she'd seen Anastasia vanish into less than a minute ago. Were they with her? Was that it? Everyone talked about the woman who could wield source energy and travelled with a demon. Was it now multiple demons?

With the pressure in her head increasing and unconsciousness threatening to wash over her like a crashing wave, Katja changed her strategy.

Ever since the air spell first stopped her from drawing breath, Katja had been trying to fight against it; to repel the spell with one of her own. Now, as her head felt like it might explode if she didn't take a breath soon, she thrust outward with a fire spell. Launching it with uncontrolled abandon from both hands, she hit the demons to her left and right with a searing blast.

In the side street just a few metres away, Anastasia jerked. What felt like a furnace door opening lit the air behind her and a shockwave of energy made her stumble forward. It almost cost her life, a loss of balance throwing her toward Aksel as he swung his sword.

She'd already tagged him twice, opening wounds on his chest and left arm. The demon had tried to use hellfire to distract her or knock her off balance, but Anastasia had simply thrown it back at him with interest.

His swings had been getting more erratic, more … panicked. Now, as she flinched away from his sweeping blade and lost her footing, she saw the look in his eyes; he was going to kill her. She couldn't stop herself from falling; the pavement was going to knock the breath from her and all he needed to do was reverse his swing. He would skewer her to the ground and take the armour and sword back to Beelzebub along with her corpse.

Whatever had caused the blast of flame and heat that filled the mouth of the narrow side street, it had changed the tide of their fight.

Tumbling, Anastasia tried to twist, attempting to bring the God Sword around to parry the thrust she knew was coming. The tip hit the ground first, denying her any form of defence and she hit the cold, damp stone with her right shoulder.

Rolling hard to her left, Aksel's death blow missed her throat, but skewered the soft flesh of her left shoulder where a piece of the armour she was still to find left her body exposed.

A scream of agony exploded from Ana's lips even through her clenched teeth. Her eyes locked on Aksel's, madness driving the comment that formed in her brain, but as she pushed the first syllable from her mouth, he vanished.

Not vanished as in he disappeared from sight, but vanished as in the sneering snarl on his face exited stage-left at such a rapid pace it was as if he had ceased to exist.

Doing her best to avoid whimpering as she rolled to her side to get up, Anastasia glanced in the direction Aksel had gone. The demon was still tumbling, pursued by a dumpster that clattered and rolled in Aksel's wake.

He'd been hit with a dumpster.

Flicking her head to see where it had come from and readying hellfire in her limp left hand rather than release her grip on the God Sword, Anastasia turned to face the figure staggering into the mouth of the alley.

It was the girl she saw earlier, the teenager with the dark hair and outfit that made her look like she was on a night out with her friends. Smoke rose from her hair and clothing, and could she see … ?

Staring at the girl, Ana asked, "Are you on fire?"

Katja followed Anastasia's eyes, looking down at her ruined outfit. "Little bit," she mumbled, patting out the smouldering hem of her favourite jacket.

Anastasia recognised the accent; German or possibly Austrian, was an easy one to spot, but she felt no need to question the girl's origins.

"That blast was you?"

Katja gave up on her clothes – they were trash. "Yup. Were those your demons?" she asked, warily watching the terrorist she'd been sent to collect. "The ones I just incinerated?"

Anastasia hooked an eyebrow. She was leaking blood. Quite steadily, in fact, and needed Daniel, the wretched coward, to heal her. It was a skill she was yet to master, and if he didn't come back for her, she was going to be stuck in Louisiana and would have to figure out the wound for herself.

"My demons? Why would any demons be mine?"

Katja slowly drew in more ley line energy. Toasting the demons had worked but almost flash-fried her at the same time. The wall of sun-level heat she threw at them would have cooked her had she not reflexively shielded herself with a swiftly conjured cold air spell. Even so it had crisped her clothing and her exposed skin felt like a bad case of sunburn.

The demons wouldn't be down for long, she expected, but perhaps long enough for the rest of the SIA teams to catch up to her. They could overpower Anastasia Aaronson and take her back to the SIA headquarters before her helpers recovered. Without a demon to open a portal, Katja suspected she might be trapped where she was.

However, the scene before her failed to gel with the information she'd been fed.

"They say you travel with a demon," Katja accused. "Are they wrong?" She tilted her head to one side, challenging Anastasia to deny it since the evidence of demons was all around her.

"No. They are right. What else do they say? That I'm dangerous? That's also correct."

Katja's attention split. The battered form of the demon she hit with the dumpster was getting to his feet, but just as her feet rose from the ground, a fresh spell forming in her hands, Anastasia whipped out her right hand.

The black sword the British woman had been so tightly holding clattered to the ground noisily and something Katja's eyes couldn't track whipped down the alley.

It struck the demon in the chest, knocking the wind out of him, but only momentarily for in the next instant he lit up from within.

There was a thin, shiny chain connecting the dagger now lodged in the demon's flesh with the handle Anastasia still held and she was driving source energy through it.

Momentarily frozen by indecision, Katja was shocked to see the demon's skin blacken. In the next second, hellfire spewed from his mouth, ears, and eyes and then he fell backward, turning to dust before his body could hit the ground.

With a twitch of her arm, Anastasia brought the weapon whipping back to the handle and in a move that looked practiced, almost like a gunslinger of old twirling a pistol before holstering it, the tiny woman slipped it back into a scabbard on the armour and reached down to retrieve the sword.

Katja hit her with lightning.

Chapter 19

It took just more than two hours for Zac and his team to get to the perimeter fence of the SIA headquarters. Carlo had settled down and though he hadn't outwardly admitted the need to include Zac, 'the outsider', he had been wise enough to cease arguing that the giant shifter might be the cause of last night's SIA raid.

The SIA Headquarters sat to the north of Rome and, while technically still inside the city limits, was well outside of the residential areas.

From the hillside looking down over the floodlit compound it looked quiet. From the outside there was no indication that there were close to sixty unwilling prisoners being held.

"Do you even have a plan?" Carlo challenged.

Without bothering to look his way, Zac fired back, "Do you?"

They were lying flat on the grass - eight shifters; all that remained of the pack. The SIA compound was before them; dark and quiet and either inviting or foreboding depending on one's particular standpoint.

Zac wasn't questioning his motivation: there were people to help, and they were his kind of people. He had no love for the SIA and had made that abundantly clear on every occasion he'd ever run into them. Maybe they were fighting for a good cause, but that gave them no right to demand he play by their rules or join their little army.

Tonight, just like they had when they first captured him, they had taken Rocco's family and pack by force. It made them the bad guys in Zac's book and though he didn't want to kill anyone, he wasn't going to feel bad if a few members of the SIA got hurt.

Performing a press-up before bouncing into a crouch, Zac sucked some air between his teeth, nodded his head, a gesture to himself rather than anyone else, and set off down the hill toward the fence line.

Watching him with a deep frown creasing his forehead, Carlo asked, "Where the hell is he going? He's going to alert the guards before we can come up with a strategy."

He was looking at Rocco when he asked it, happy to blame the alpha's son for involving the giant werewolf in the first place.

Hearing the question and knowing no one could give a better answer than he, Zac spoke over his shoulder. "I'm taking a straight line toward the main doors. When I get there, I'm going to politely ask where they put the people they took tonight."

Someone asked, "Is he kidding?"

Zac just continued talking. "If they don't wish to assist me with my enquiry. I'll ask again. A bit more insistently."

To remove any ambiguity about what that might entail, Zac tore off his shirt and transformed, the shift from one form to the next taking less than a second. With a flex of his muscular arms, it was complete, his skin now shining like onyx under the moon.

He turned, walking crab-like as he asked, "You coming? Or what?" Another flex, this time of his left arm, brought the shield to life and a swing of his right arm cleaved the fence apart so he didn't even break stride as he walked through it.

None of the pack moved, each of them watching Zac's back as he strolled across the grass inside the compound and onto the car park. Then, like a surging wave, when the first of them started to move, the rest followed in quick succession, men and women discarding their clothes as they transformed into their supernatural forms.

Zac had spent several minutes watching the activity in the SIA compound. Nothing much was happening. There wasn't even a patrol to check the perimeter that he could see. No guard towers to watch the land surrounding the compound ... But why would there be? Until tonight, he doubted it had ever housed more than a few prisoners, if any. They had no reason to expect an attack by a hostile force so had made no preparation to defend against it.

Their complacency played into Zac's hands, and he was almost all the way to the main entrance when he was finally spotted.

Exiting the building were six of the SIA agents drawn into the previous evening's operation. None of them had been tasked with capturing the werewolf pack, but five of the six were themselves supernaturals and all believed in what they were doing.

They reacted in shock. It had been a long day that led into an unexpected evening and then to a long night that crept into the early hours before it was deemed tenable for them to be released. Half the agents involved in the enforced recruitment op were still in the building – there were so many captives to manage, so the six now facing Zachary had been racing from the building before someone higher could call them back.

With a snarl, Zachary leapt. Imbued with both supernatural strength and speed, his extraordinary height and size for a human made him a significantly terrifying opponent as a shifter.

Barrelling into the agents, he caught them before any could fully transform or bring their magic to bear.

In a snatched utterance of panic, a wizard called Hugo fell backward as he formed a shield. Nothing would penetrate the shield, formed as it was by pure elemental energy, but that made no difference to Zachary.

Using his own shield as a battering ram, he slammed into Hugo's defensive wall and used the exchange of energy to rebound the wizard into the doors he'd just exited.

With enough force to shatter glass, Hugo's body hit the right-hand door and went through it to send a shower of tiny crystalline pieces across the tiled floor beyond.

An alarm sprang to life, activated by someone inside.

Zac didn't even slow down. Now that his presence was obvious, the people on the other side of the glass doors were reacting. Humans, or normos, as many of the supers were now calling non-supernatural people, were reaching for guns, shifters were shifting, and wizards/witches were readying spells.

There weren't enough of them though and Zachary had the element of surprise. Smashing through the glass, he let the shield do precisely what it was designed for. Knowing that no one would conjure lightning or fire in such a confined space, Zac anticipated air spells and was unsurprised when he felt his throat constricting.

Someone was trying to shut off his air supply. It was a sound tactic, but it failed to address a major issue – he was going to slap the sense out of whoever was wielding the spell long before it could be effective.

Being careful to keep his claws tucked in, he did precisely that, blocking attacks on one side with the shield while taking the fight out of anyone within slapping distance on the other.

Someone fired a spell in his direction, employing lightning to defy Zachary's assumptions. It knocked out the lights in the lobby, plunging it into darkness. With a pop and fizzle, the electrics shorted out though, annoyingly, the alarm continued to wail.

Zac spun and struck, pirouetting neatly into a semi-crouch as he looked around for anyone left to fight.

In less than seven seconds, he was the only one in the SIA Head-quarters lobby still standing, and the rest of the pack were only just arriving.

TJ stepped over the threshold, the glass crunching beneath the boots he still wore, to find Carlo and the others looking around at the unconscious SIA agents lying on the cool tile. He watched as Zachary lifted one from the floor by the front of his shirt.

"Hey. Where are you keeping the people you took tonight?" He had to shout to be heard over the alarm.

Getting no answer, he dropped the figure, the man's head making a dull thunk sound when it hit the tile. Moving to the next agent, he tried again with the same result.

"Maybe keep one conscious next time?" Carlo remarked, winning a point.

Zac dropped the agent he was holding and started toward a bank of elevators.

"Sure. You can lead the next attack. You can show me how it's done."

At the elevators, Zac delicately extended the claw on his pinky finger to carefully press the call button.

"We're taking the elevator?" questioned Joshua. "Won't that trap us? Anyway, we don't know what floor they are on, do we?" He checked around to see if he had missed a vital piece of information.

Zac shook his head and shoved open the door to the stairs.

"Your friends and family will be in the basement, at least a few floors down where ley lines don't penetrate. They do that to stop the wizards conjuring magic to escape. Not that it works as well as they think it should." Zac remembered Otto Schneider figuring out how to escape when the SIA first incarcerated him. "And yes, the elevator would make for a great kill box. Only a fool would use one."

Chapter 20

Torn from the ground just as her fingers grasped the hilt of the sword, Anastasia's vision was filled with nothing but white as all her senses fired at once. The pain the lightning inflicted was excruciating, but the suit of armour protected her from the worst of it.

A single thought filled her head: *I need that shield.*

Katja was already throwing a second spell, conjuring the earth to trap her target. Maybe Anastasia wasn't the terrorist everyone said she was, and maybe she was. It was all too much for a fifteen-year-old to figure out. Faced with the opportunity to capture her, Katja was doing what was expected of her.

The demons were bad. Anastasia Aaronson was probably working with them. Capturing her to get answers sounded like a good plan.

However, focused on the mortal to her front, Katja had forgotten the two to her rear.

Acadus and Bitrius never saw Katja's inferno coming and had suffered accordingly, their skin burned away by the intensity of the flame she produced. However, the magic that kept them immortal was already healing them before the heat died away.

The remaining five teams of SIA agents had converged in the street drawn by Wanda's final messages only to find not the one demon they believed to be travelling with their target, but two, and they had captured Katja.

The sight of Acadus and Bitrius – known by those agents who were former familiars, was enough to make the two of them flee. They opened portals and returned to the SIA headquarters too terrified to even attempt to face two of the four horsemen. If two were in plain sight, then the other two had to be around somewhere close by.

No one knew Anastasia had killed Martha.

The rest of the SIA agents, most of whom were unaware of Wanda's fate or that two of their force had just bugged out, attempted to trade blows.

It was a futile effort; mortal elemental magic is like pitching a Sunday dad's league against a premiership team of professional sportsmen, yet they were not going to abandon Katja who they could see was held by one of the demons as he continued to fling hellfire around.

When Katja vanished inside a ball of flame, those looking her way found their vision blurred by the abrupt white light and no one saw where she went. Urgent radio messages back and forth confirmed no one had eyes on the teenage girl and no one could see their target, Anastasia Aaronson, either.

The moments of hasty discussion that followed, no one wanting to be the first to step into the open, played right into the demons' hands as the magic inside them worked to repair the damage wrought by the young German girl.

In the side street, fighting to stay on her feet, Anastasia gasped a lungful of air.

"Little girl. I have no wish to hurt you."

Katja had no wish to hurt her opponent either, but if she was dangerous, she had to be stopped. Intending to hit Ana with the same manipulation of an air spell that had cut off her ability to breath just a few minutes ago, her eyes flared when she saw the wanted supernatural terrorist snatch at her throwing dagger again.

She had lied! Anastasia was everything they said she was!

On impulse, as the knife flew toward her, Katja changed her spell, pushing a wave of air outward to alter the knife's trajectory. It was like pushing against the wind itself, the blade moving too fast and the surface area too small for Katja to have any real effect. So it came as a surprise when it shot past her anyway.

It had never been aimed at her, Katja realised, twisted in the air to see the two barbequed demons entering the alley behind her.

Anastasia screamed in frustration as the knife missed its target, Katja's conjuring doing enough to disrupt her aim.

Both demons formed hellfire orbs in their hands, their swords gone now; melted and warped by the heat of Katja's fire spell.

The throwing dagger zipped back on its chain to reach Ana's hand once more, but before she could take aim again, Bitrius opened a portal.

The last two horsemen stepped through it, loosing their hellfire orbs as a parting gesture though they dwindled to nothing with a wave of Katja's hand.

Silence filled the side street, both women staring at the point where the portal had been until the sound of running feet and shouted messages reached their ears.

Katja turned to face Anastasia and descended until her feet touched the ground, allowing the ley line energy in her body to dwindle – effectively disarming herself.

"That was impressive," Ana commented, frowning a little in her surprise and also from the light-headedness she now felt from her loss of blood. Using the God Sword as a cane to keep herself upright, she added, "The thing with the hellfire. How did you do that?"

Katja shrugged. "Honestly, I'm still trying to work that out. I guess I sort of see the energy inside of it as a part of the earth – its physical makeup or something like that, and I return the energy to the world."

It was an answer, but not one that provided Anastasia with anything she understood.

"What are you?" Katja asked.

It was Ana's turn to shrug, a sad smile tugging at her mouth. "No one seems to know the answer to that one. Is it your friends I can hear coming?"

Katja nodded. "Will you come with me? The SIA believe you are dangerous. That you are working against the interests of humanity. If that's not true, you should join us." She saw Anastasia wince. It wasn't the first time. The front of her clothing was slick with blood from a wound to her shoulder. "That looks pretty bad. Maybe you should let us help you." She took a step forward, her arms open wide to show she had no spells conjured and ready.

Anastasia felt a little sick. Woozy from the blood loss, she wanted nothing more than to be around people again. It would be so great to be a part of something, to have colleagues to fight alongside, but she had met the head of the SIA. There was no way he would listen to her.

They would want the armour, they would take the sword, and they would lock her up if she refused to cooperate. She was as certain of that as she was the need to keep gathering the pieces of armour.

She was the only being to have killed a demon in over four thousand years. Maybe she was the only one who would ever be able to do so. There was something unique about her. Anastasia had no idea what it was, she hadn't asked for it, but what if she was the only one who could stop Beelzebub?

The approaching footsteps changed in tone and volume as two young women reached the end of the narrow side street and skidded into view.

"Katja!" gasped Cassie, shocked to see the German girl alive. At her side, Jennifer wasted no time speaking.

Confused enough by Katja's ability to dismantle hellfire even as it was being thrown around, Ana's brow creased again to see the two girls, clearly twins, enveloped in a bright yet ethereal light. They were conjuring, the spell in their hands dripping golden sparks, yet though it was two of them forming it, the spell acted as if it had one life.

Katja screamed, "Noooo!" Facing the twins and shouting for them to cease. Too late the spell released, but whatever it was going to do, Anastasia never got to find out.

An arm snaked around her waist, yanking her backward and she tumbled through a portal, the scent of Daniel's cologne filling her nostrils as she fell against his chest.

Chapter 21

"Sir, there are supernaturals storming the lobby!" The report, delivered in a panicked tone, came from one of Director Alpi's lieutenants, but it wasn't news. He already knew they were under attack – everyone in the compound knew they were under attack because the alarm had sounded, and they had a few seconds of footage from the camera in the lobby before someone loosed a spell that knocked out the feed.

"Stop panicking!" Alpi commanded, his voice a roar that demanded immediate calm from everyone within ear shot. "I saw shifters. It's likely to be the friends or family of those we took tonight. They mounted a rescue attempt and I applaud their bravery." Alpi spun slowly, making eye contact with as many of his agents as possible. It was clear from their expression they held a different opinion.

"Sir, we can lock this level down," reported Lieutenant Foggarty, settling in front of a computer to access the door controls. "That will hold them until reinforcements get here."

Alpi's voice boomed again. "Do not touch that computer, Foggarty!"

Most of the agents in the room were already looking his way, but Alpi's latest order drew the attention of every last soul.

"We are going to draw them in and corner them. This will complete tonight's operation nicely. More volunteers for Ironbolt's Army. We shall remove that which is drawing the demons to our great city, and show everyone that Italy leads the way in defending the world." A sea of shocked faces looked back at him. "Are you afraid?" Alpi questioned. "They are shifters. Most of you are wizards." He narrowed his eyes at a tall African woman. "Gana, you are a former familiar for heaven's sake. What do you have to fear from a few shifters? We are going to let them in and then shut the door so they cannot get out." The incredulous expressions aimed his way deepened. "This is the job, people! We are at war with the demons and the SIA needs powerful supernaturals to fight that war. Do you want to face the demon horde alone when it comes? Or would you like some reinforcements? That's who is heading your way right now – reinforcements. If you cannot see that, then you are blind. Now get to it. I want the shifters subdued the moment they come inside the room. Do the thing with their air supply," Alpi mimed strangling himself with his left hand. "Take them as peacefully as possible."

For a moment he thought he might have to bark at the room to spark some movement and was glad to be saved the need to do so by the flurry of activity that erupted just as he was drawing his next breath.

In truth, it worried him that a small force of shifters could so easily enter his building. The SIA headquarters wasn't designed to be a fortress – an oversight that he would discuss with Ironbolt and others in the morning. How many of his agents must they have already overpowered?

A handful? More than a dozen? Shifters were known for their power and aggression, but on balance a wizard should always win. That was the opinion he'd been fed. As a vanilla human, Director Alpi had no experience to draw on, not that he would let such a minor deficit in his knowledge base impact his decisions.

"Sir." Captain Benigni approached, his face failing to hide that he wanted to raise what he already knew was going to be a controversial subject.

Alpi made it clear he felt Benigni ought to have something else he should be doing.

"Yes? What is it?"

Alpi saw the doubt in Captain Benigni's eyes. It made him question if the man had perhaps already been promoted beyond his level of ability.

Benigni licked his lips nervously.

"Well, Sir, I wondered … if perhaps we ought to request immediate assistance."

Alpi hiked an eyebrow, encouraging Benigni to keep talking.

"Well, the base in America. They have many, many former familiars, Sir. They could be here in seconds … it's daylight there …" His words petered out under the glare of his commander.

"Let me see if I have this right," Alpi remarked in a mocking tone. "On the cusp of capturing a group of shifters displaying all the talents we most desire: bravery, determination, teamwork … you want to tell the world we cannot manage. You wish to announce to the president of the SIA, my boss, that the Italians need help to put down a small, undisciplined rabble?"

"Well …"

"I'm going to advance to you the small amount of goodwill I have left and pretend this conversation never happened, Benigni. Go away."

The captain scurried back to his desk, and Alpi saw him give a small shake of his head when several sets of eyes looked his way. Benigni was even weaker than he had first believed. The man wasn't even speaking for himself, but had been pressured into approaching the boss by his subordinates.

Feeling calm and in control, Director Alpi surveyed his domain. The instruction to recall the agents already released from duty had been enacted. They were overdue some down time, not least because he needed them to replace those who stayed on. Everyone was working overtime and that wasn't going to let up any time soon. It was unfortunate his overworked agents had to be recalled so soon after such a long shift, but he wasn't going to call for outside help.

The gang of shifters, however many there were, would arrive soon to find there was never any chance they could reach their brethren. They would be subdued, and once they were incarcerated, he would calmly address them, praising them for their 'misguided' endeavour. They would join the SIA as cannon fodder not because they were being forced to do so, but because it was the right thing to do. The world needed them. Humanity, supernaturals included, would stand together against the impending demon invasion or they would all fail together.

So far as Alpi could see, it was one or the other.

His musings were cut off when the sound of footsteps echoed in the stairwell. They were in the third level basement, three floors above the hastily converted floor where the captured supernaturals were being kept. All around him, wizards and witches began to conjure spells, the sparks coming from their hand actions lighting the air.

Chapter 22

Ana wanted to push away from Daniel. He'd abandoned her to fight the horsemen alone and suddenly returning to rescue her had created a rush of rage. If she possessed the energy in her to do so, she would slap his face.

With an armoured gauntlet.

However, blood loss, the pain of her injury, and exhaustion from the effort of battle had drained her resistance. She needed him. He could heal her and keep her safe.

Then she was going to slap him.

"I'm sorry," Daniel's voice whispered in her ear.

She replied with an insult.

"Yes," he whispered again, gently lowering her to the floor. "I deserve that. I ... I panicked, I think. It's a new concept for me. I've never felt afraid before ... well, until recently, I guess."

To Anastasia's ears the confession came as a shock. It felt like she'd known the demon for most of her life, which was kind of true. She met him only months ago, but her memories had been completely reset only months before that when the piece of shrapnel ripped through her brain. The point, of course, was that until this very moment, Daniel had always been secretive, closed off. He never talked about how he felt; it just wasn't something a demon would do.

A million responses came and went without being aired; none of them sounded right in her head. He was healing her, and she was on a bed again, the soft, supportive comfort of a quality mattress taking away some of the aches as Daniel manipulated source energy to heal her wounds.

Eventually, she asked, "Where are we?" The room was dark, but she could see two sash windows along the wall to her right and the room possessed a high ceiling. Painted in white, the furnishings and décor gave a sense of opulence.

"Balmoral Castle."

Anastasia blinked, the word echoing in her head until she spasmed and tried to sit up.

"Balmoral! Argh. Ow. Oh, God that hurt." She laid back down on the bed covers. "Are we really in Balmoral?"

Daniel's attention was focused on healing Anastasia's wounds, and he did not look up when he said, "Yes. Why?"

A snigger escaped Ana's lips. "Because it's the Queen's house, dummy. I'm sure the Queen of England means very little to a demon, but it's a big deal for me."

"Well, she's sleeping two rooms along from you right now if you want to meet her."

"WHAT!" Ana tensed her stomach muscles to sit up again, but remembered how much it hurt the last time and relaxed them before attempting to rise. "The problem with you, Daniel, is that I never know when you are lying and when you are being honest."

"I am rarely honest, Anastasia."

"Ain't that the truth."

"However, this time I can assure you the Queen of England is indeed less than twenty feet from you. I opened a portal into her room first by accident when I was looking for a safe place to go."

Lying still and letting Daniel work his, quite literal, magic, Anastasia wondered what someone like the Queen might say to her when all this was done. Would the Queen survive the demon invasion? Could she, a five-foot-one-inch woman with missing limbs, manage to stop Beelzebub when he came? What about Godfrey, Beelzebub's brother, and the angels? She hadn't heard anything from them in weeks. Benjamin ... her thoughts turned to Benjamin – whatever had become of him?

She could only hide from her thoughts when it came to him.

The pain in her shoulder had already subsided and when she pressed her chin against her collar bone to look at the wound site, she could see fresh pink skin where the hole in her flesh had been.

Daniel moved away, crossing the room to look out onto the moonlit gardens.

Sitting up, Anastasia rolled her shoulder, checking for tightness or residual pain. There was none. His ability to heal her was nothing short of miraculous and undoubtedly one of the reasons why ancient humans had come to look at his race as deities to be worshipped and exalted.

Sliding off the bed to check her appearance in the mirror, she announced, "We need to go back to Mostar. I have to find the shield." She wanted the helmet too and all the rest of the missing pieces from the armour suit, but the shield was at the top of her list. With it she imagined her recent battles would have been far more easily won. "What time is it there, now? No, sorry, forget I asked." Anastasia already knew the time difference to Croatia was two hours.

It was one of the odd quirks with her brain injury: she had a bunch of things she knew, but had no memory of learning them. Had she holidayed in Croatia? Was that how she knew? Dismissing the question, she repeated her previous statement.

"We need to go."

"It will be light there in just a few hours. It would be better to move with the sun, not against it."

"You can drop me off and come back for me. We both have phones, right?"

Daniel turned away from the window, eyeing his companion with a look that Anastasia could not read. Was he unhappy that she wanted to ditch him? Did he fear for her safety? She doubted the latter because that was laughable – in Louisiana he ran for his life and left her to fend for herself. Plus, she had a suit of armour … well, most of a suit, and a sword that could kill an immortal. Who was going to challenge her?

To Ana's surprise, Daniel said, "Okay. If that is what you want."

She almost asked what he would do while she was in Mostar hunting for information on the shield, but bit her tongue. It didn't matter what he did. He had to stay out of the sun, so until the darkness fell on Croatia many hours later, she would be on her own and stuck there. It seemed more prudent to worry about herself.

The almost nothing sound of Daniel opening a portal brought her eyes up.

"Ready?" he asked, poised to step through. The portal wasn't going to Mostar, of course, but to the immortal realm from where he could then open a second one to take her to wherever she wanted to go.

It was daylight on the other side, a dawn-like glow of gentle sun that one sees on an early spring morning. In the immortal realm, the demons could tolerate the sun, a fact no one could explain.

Ana took Daniel's hand and stepped from one realm to the next only to do the same again to a darkened street in Mostar a moment later.

She recognised where she was instantly – it had only been a short time since she was last here looking for the shield.

Alex would have told her if she'd been able to find any better information about the shield's location, so now it was time to put on her sleuthing hat and ask some questions. Someone had to know what had happened to it.

Chapter 23

A cadus and Bitrius were in private audience with Beelzebub in his palace. Much like Daniel, the concept of fear was a new one, but the probability of death at Anastasia Aaronson's hands had been enough to make them flee. They both silently accepted it and would have never talked about it again had Beelzebub not been waiting for them upon their return.

He had spies, that was the underlying problem to negotiate. The lord of hell knew everything because shilt, demons, and other creatures in his domain were more than happy to provide him with information in promise of favour.

A messenger had been waiting for them upon their return to the immortal realm, the instruction a simple one: report to Beelzebub.

Acadus kept his voice even and confident when he spoke. "She possesses more than half of the armour, my lord."

Bitrius quickly added his voice, "We believed we could return both it and the weapons she holds to you, master."

"And yet you return with neither," Beelzebub observed coldly.

Acadus opened his mouth, closing it again when he realised he had nothing to say that would make him sound anything other than weak.

They were standing in one of the central rooms within Beelzebub's palace – standing not sitting which would have been their usual stance. That their master had been clear about their need to remain standing was an indication of how low they had fallen in his eyes.

Beelzebub had four generals who commanded battalions of demons and above them sat the four horsemen, the name coined when the demons learned of the legends that persisted among the mortals.

It was amusing that the humans half remembered their former masters, yet had everything wrong.

Ever since the death curse began to fade and the possibility of a permanent return to earth became a reality, Beelzebub had been talking about the battle that would come. Humanity was raping the planet on a daily basis, destroying it like a child who has outgrown their toys. The demons would seize control once more, sweeping aside the humans' insignificant resistance to rule again. For almost a millennia, Beelzebub had planned and prepared.

Now though, in the last few decades, humans were developing magic of their own. It was first detected almost five hundred years ago, but was so weak and so unworthy of attention that few had bothered with it. Only Daniel, a low caste demon had sought to leverage his position by finding a way to bring humans back to the immortal realm. They made good familiars, their feeble magical skills notwithstanding, but they grew stronger and more capable.

It was seen as an advantage – there would be humans worth saving when they ruled over them, and they could cherry pick those not to be culled.

However, in just the last few years, something had changed. The rate at which the number of humans developed or discovered a spark of magic within themselves exploded, growing at an almost exponential rate. Among them, though the majority were weak, some possessed extraordinary power. The girl, Katja Weber, and Anastasia Aaronson were just two of them. Otto Schneider's power was less than theirs and different, but that he had absorbed Teague's immortality made him equally dangerous.

They numbered just a few, and would fall against the might of the demon horde, led by creatures the humans could not imagine. Nevertheless, their master, Beelzebub, appeared to show concern.

"With every failed encounter, every time you or any of my subjects goes up against a human only to lose, you increase their ability to hope." Bitrius and Acadus remained silent, listening while their lord lectured. "Hope will make them fight, and make no mistake, they will fight. I hear they are forming an army. A global coalition that intends to stand against us."

"We will crush them under our boot, my lord," Acadus remarked with confidence.

The back-handed slap to his face sent him across the room, fetching against a wall where he slumped, staring at Beelzebub with shocked eyes.

"Yes, we will, you fool. That is the problem. The finest of the humans. The ones who would serve us best in the new world will die, killed because they left us no choice. And why?" Beelzebub's voice raised to a crescendo. "Because you gave them hope!"

Bitrius dropped to his knees, prostrating himself before his master when he asked, "What must we do, Lord? How can we redeem ourselves?"

Beelzebub kicked the demon with a lazy foot, sending him sprawling across the floor because Bitrius offered no resistance.

"Stop begging for a start, you simpering fool. The four horsemen were mighty. Look at yourselves now. Two of your number slain by a mortal girl with a knife. Go. Leave my house. I will call for you when I have need.

Chapter 24

Encountering no resistance in the stairwell as they descended could only mean one thing.

"It's a trap?" questioned TJ.

Zachary nodded his head. "Almost certainly. They will be waiting for us to flood the lower levels and probably intend to trap us there."

TJ looked at Joshua. The pack were lined up on the stairs behind Zachary, all of them more than happy to let him go first – no one else had a giant magical shield to keep them safe. They stretched back to the next landing, the less confident hanging back to let the braver, or perhaps more foolhardy, go ahead.

"So what do we do?" asked Joshua.

Zac frowned as if he failed to understand the question.

"We attack as previously discussed."

TJ raised his hand, then pulled it back to his waist again when he realised how foolish he looked.

"What about the part where it's a trap?"

"Yeah," echoed Joshua and maybe half a dozen others.

Zac shrugged, a gesture that demonstrated the girth of his trapezius muscles.

"I don't see how that changes anything. Unless of course you no longer wish to rescue your family and friends." It wasn't aired as a question, though technically it sounded like one, but no one got to respond because Zachary chose that moment to charge.

Gripping the banister with his right hand, he leapt out into the void and down through the centre of the stairs. Dropping a floor and a half, he hit the landing below, bent his legs to absorb the impact and converted his upward thrust to explode forward.

If he needed any further proof that he was being led into a trap, the door on this level was open.

It was dark beyond, and the weak, ethereal light coming from his shield did nothing to illuminate the black spaces as he charged through the doorway. Behind him, the pack were roaring as they came, a war cry to bolster their spirits and charge their hearts with the courage to face their opponents.

It was all over in thirty seconds.

There was a truth to Director Alpi's remark that a wizard, on balance, will always beat a shifter. Shifters are hard to beat; their skin hardens, and their speed and strength dictate that they can shrug off a lot of punishment. However, wizards have a lot more tools in their box.

A wily mage can manipulate the elements to defeat a shifter despite the physical superiority unless they fail to anticipate what a shifter will do or react too slowly.

On this occasion, it made no difference what Alpi's subordinates planned to do. Not because Zac and the pack following hard on his heels were too fast and too numerous to stop, but because Gana, the former familiar, worked a spell that she aimed at her colleagues and not the attacking werewolves.

Charging into the room, his shield high to deflect lightning or blunt objects hurled by an air manipulation, Zac searched for the nearest SIA agent. Like before, he would only hurt them if he had to and had his claws tucked in for their safety. He was not a killer by nature.

There was no one to attack and he skidded to a stop a quarter of a way across the large room. The finely attuned hearing and sense of smell he possessed as a werewolf told him there were people in the room. More than three dozen of them, yet no opposition came, and none were even in sight.

Spotting a pair of boots sticking out from behind a desk, his eyebrows pinched together.

The pack, having run down the stairs rather than leap over them to plummet forty feet, arrived on the same level and spewed through the door still roaring their banshee cry. It petered out when they found Zachary standing over an unconscious form.

Rocco gasped, "Wow. That was fast. I told you this guy could fight."

Perplexed, Zac said, "It wasn't me."

"No, it was me." A tall, thin woman with a rounded face stepped out from behind a pillar, her arms extended and her hands open. "Are you Zachary?" she asked.

Zac's eyebrows unpinched and shot skywards.

"Um, yes. Um, how do you know me? I didn't ... um. I didn't sleep with you and never call, did I?"

Gana tittered quietly, enjoying seeing the giant shifter squirm.

"I know Otto Schneider," she revealed. "He talks about you sometimes."

Relaxing his stance and allowing the shield to vanish back inside his body where it magically stored itself until needed, Zac said, "I hope it's all good things."

His remark brought another giggle.

"No, he refers to you as an annoying oaf. He also says you are the best man he has ever known and that you have a heart that makes humanity worth saving."

Puzzling over the contrasting elements of her report, Zac finally went with, "Thank you. I think. What happened here?"

Around him, the pack had filled the room and were examining the fallen SIA agents.

Abruptly, Carlo raged, "I know this one!" he was lifting a man from the floor by his lapels. "He took my cousins, Irina and Judas." His outstretched hand, claws extended was about to plunge downward when Rocco caught it.

Incensed, Carlo ripped his head around to snarl at the younger man.

Zac picked up a chair and threw it. The blow it delivered to Carlo was glancing but it got his attention just as other pack members were converging on him.

"No one hurts anyone," Zac stated bluntly. There was to be no arguing.

From across the room, Gana said, "That's precisely what I mean: you have every right to storm this place and take revenge for yesterday's actions, which, guiltily, I took part in. Now I need to put them right. I need to put them right because they were wrong. Otto Schneider didn't rescue me from demon slavery so I could oppress supernaturals in this realm. The world might need an army, but this is not the way to go about it."

Carlo opened his hand, dropping the unconscious man to the floor but continued to glare at Rocco, the pack alpha's son while he did so. TJ, Joshua, and more were within touching distance, their gazes enough to make Carlo move away, though no one thought that particular encounter was truly over.

"You could choose to hurt the people I rendered unconscious, but you won't, will you, Zachary?"

Zachary shrugged again. "Where are the prisoners?"

Chapter 25

I t was the middle of the night, and the cathedral was locked as Anastasia expected it would be. Dawn was hours away, but she was not in the mood to wait.

Fetching her phone from a back pocket and shocked to find it was still in one piece and functioning, she called Alex.

Her librarian friend answered, but only after the phone had gone to voice mail and Ana killed the call and tried again.

"Ana? God, what time is it?"

"In Mostar? Nearly four in the morning. Sorry to wake you, but I'm here and I need help to track down someone who might be able to point me in the right direction to find the shield. I just got my ass kicked by the four horsemen again."

Sleepily, and around a yawn, Alex managed, "Don't you mean, three horsemen."

A smile spread across Ana's face. "Two now, actually. I killed Aksel. I think I might have got the others too if they hadn't chickened out. They escaped through a portal. Anyway," Ana skipped back to the subject at hand; there would be time for stories and stuff if they survived, "I need help to find the shield. I've no idea how long it's been missing."

"Ah, well ... Well done on killing Aksel, by the way. That's an odd statement, isn't it? I'm a library research assistant. Or I would be if I had a position at a library anywhere, and here I am congratulating you on ending someone's life."

Ana skewed her lips to one side, accepting Alex's comments on the matter.

"That's the world we live in now."

"Yes. Was it spectacular like when you killed Martha?"

"I'm not sure I would use the world spectacular ..."

Daniel made a show of tapping his wrist – he had a limited window to hang around in Mostar with her. Then the sun was going to come up.

"Sorry, Alex, I really don't have time to chat," Anastasia tried once again to steer her friend back to the topic of choice. A voice in the background said something and a muffled version of Alex's voice – like she had just put her hand over the phone - replied. "Who was that?" Ana snapped. "Alex are you in trouble? Tap the phone and I'll be there in ten seconds!" She was already grabbing Daniel's arm and about to demand he open a portal.

Hissing into Ana's ear, Alex said, "Shhhh. It's a guy, okay? I'm not made of stone. I do have to eat and ... stuff. I went out and ... well, you can fill in the rest."

Anastasia blushed. Then, catching herself blushing and embarrassed about being embarrassed for no good reason, she mumbled, "Right, okay. Good for you, I guess."

"Yes, it was, thank you. Now listen. I managed to find a report from 1992. The war in the former Republic of Yugoslavia had spread to Mostar and the city was heavily bombarded for several days. That's probably when the column was damaged – you said there was a hollow column?"

"That's right."

"Okay, well that's likely when they found it because I looked at records of bishops and other clergy associated with the cathedral and there were three new appointments all within a short stretch of time in 1992."

"You think that could be when they found the shield?" Ana's memory flashed to Rochester Cathedral when she found the sword and the elderly verger who died picking it up.

Alex's reply came back instantly, "That would be my guess. I managed to find a record of staff currently employed, but I couldn't find anything to say how long they have been there. So given that it's been thirty years, I've ruled out anyone under the age of fifty-five. I'm sending you a file now. Hold on."

The sound of a computer starting up and Alex's fingernails clacking across the keys met Ana's ears.

The male someone spoke again, his voice distant and unintelligible.

Alex said, "No. Go back to bed. I'll be with you shortly." Then to Ana, "There are only three probabilities ... possibilities, I guess since any of them could have started working at the cathedral after 1992. It's the best I can do, I'm afraid."

The chime of an incoming email echoed in Anastasia's ear, and she pulled the phone away from her face to check it.

"Oh, you have phone numbers and addresses."

"Yup," Alex boasted proudly. "I'm all kinds of brilliant."

"Okay. Well, I'll let you get back to ... whatever," Ana teased before thanking Alex once again and hanging up.

Daniel had moved to stand alongside Anastasia and was looking over her shoulder. "You have addresses?"

"And phone numbers," Ana replied, thumbing the first number on the list so her phone would ask if she wanted to call it.

"Yes, but you have addresses," Daniel repeated, this time as a statement as he grabbed Ana's arm and yanked her backward.

With a surprised, "Urkk!" Ana toppled off balance as the demon took her through a portal and then another to arrive in a darkened street.

"What the hell, Daniel?" she slapped his arm away. "Where are we now?"

Looking at the row of modest houses they faced, Daniel nodded his head in their direction.

"This is the first address. I've been here before. Or close by, at least. I just need to figure out which house it is." He leaned over to see the phone again.

"Or we could just call them," Anastasia frowned in disapproval of his strategy. "We can't just knock on doors at this time of the night."

Daniel snorted with derision. "And you think they will answer the phone at this time of night?"

Snapping out an arm, he grabbed her neck, making the skin contact he needed to take her through as he opened yet another portal. Bouncing them into the immortal realm and back out in the blink of an eye, they arrived inside one of the houses they were facing less than five seconds earlier.

Ana elbowed Daniel in the ribs, aiming to drive the air from his lungs and having little impact.

Looking along the darkened hallway from their position just inside the house, Daniel said, "Oh, yeah. This is much more familiar." A broad smile filled the demon's features.

"From your days kidnapping people to make them into slaves?"

Daniel's smile fell.

"Let's not reminisce, eh?" Ana hit the dial button on her phone and lifted it to her ear as somewhere in the house a phone began to ring.

"You're phoning them even though we are already in their house?"

Ignoring him, Anastasia waited for the call to connect and heard a person upstairs swearing in Croatian before the call was cut off without being answered.

She tried again, but this time it didn't ring – the phone was off now. Or on silent. Either way, she wasn't getting an answer.

Muttering under her breath, she looked up at Daniel to find a totally fake innocent expression looking back at her.

"Okay, okay. We'll do it your way," she sighed.

They were in someone else's house and though Anastasia hoped the age of the person she wanted to speak with would mean there were no children in the house, she still wasn't happy about terrorising the homeowner by bursting into his bedroom.

Of course, she did it anyway.

Shoving Daniel out of the way when he tried to lead the way, she formed sinfire in her left hand. It was mostly to provide a gentle glow of light so she wouldn't accidentally tread on something or trip, but also so that she had a line of defence if the homeowner, Novak Rossovich, if Alex's list was correct, had a gun in his nightstand.

Did they have guns as home defence in Croatia? Ana had no idea, so on a two count, she burst through what Daniel assured her was the bedroom door.

"Daniel!"

Staring at a bath, toilet, and sink, she knew the demon had deliberately duped her and spun on the spot to see his cheeky grin vanish through a doorway on the other side of the landing.

A shout of shock, warning, and fear filled the air, followed by a scream of terror made by a woman's voice.

Racing to get to them, just in case Daniel did something to shut them up, Anastasia wasn't prepared for the sight that greeted her.

Mr and Mrs Rossovich elected to sleep without clothes, so upon Daniel's entry and their shock-driven leap from bed, they were now displaying all they had to show.

Ana averted her eyes. Not because Mr Rossovich's junk was flapping about, although obviously that was a factor, but so she could give them a modicum of modesty to robe themselves.

"Daniel," Ana hissed insistently. "Douse that orb of hellfire right now."

"It's making them obedient," he argued. "Yes, I am one of those dangerous demons you have seen on TV. Do as I say, or I will drag you to hell."

Mrs Rossovich exclaimed something in Croatian and fainted backward onto the bed. Mr Rossovich, frozen by fear and unable to decide whether he should go to his wife's aid or possibly dive out of his second story window, slowly raised his hands.

"Daniel," Anastasia hissed again.

Chuckling, the demon let the hellfire reabsorb into the skin of his palm and twisted at the waist to open a wardrobe.

Throwing a shirt, he said, "Here, put this on."

Ana gave it a three count before revolving to face Mr Rossovich. He had his shirt on, but his belly pushed it out at the front to stop it falling far enough to cover any of the things she didn't wish to look at.

Giving up with a mutter, she addressed him directly for the first time.

"Mr Rossovich, are you employed by the Cathedral of the Parish of Mary Mother of the Church?"

Mr Rossovich, blinked, not understanding a word.

Swearing, Ana gripped her phone, opening the Apps App so she could find a translator to use.

Daniel simply switched to speaking Croatian.

"Pán Rossovich, ste zamestnaný v katedrále farnosti Matky Cirkvi?"

Ana's jaw dropped open, but she shut it again because the four-thousand-year-old demon's ability to speak multiple languages fluently shouldn't have been a surprise to her.

She listened, unable to follow the exchange and jumped half out of her skin when Mrs Rossovich came around, saw the demon, and filled the house with a scream that threatened to break glass.

Mrs Rossovich's eyes bugged from her head, and she jabbered in her terror until her husband cut her off with insistent shushes.

While the couple talked, his words soothing his wife though Ana felt they had every right to be terrified, Daniel explained what he had learned.

"Novak remembers the incident with great clarity; both the bomb that came through the roof of the cathedral one Tuesday night, and the discovery of the shield when they attempted to clear the rubble. He claims that five people died attempting to pick it up. It was found by builders in the aftermath of the explosion. Two of them died when they picked it out of the wreckage. Either way, he says they used tools to place it into a wooden crate. He doesn't know what happened to it after that."

Ana's next question was as instant as it was obvious. "Who does?"

Chapter 26

M uch to Anastasia's surprise, Mr Rossovich chose to help them. Whether it was from the unspoken consequence of failing to comply with Daniel's requests, or because he believed her insistence that she needed to obtain the shield for the sake of the world, she could not tell.

To prove her point, Anastasia had shown him and his wife the suit of armour and the sword which she pushed sinfire through so it lit up impressively. It was a convincing enough display to make them back away.

Mr Rossovich used his phone to call a colleague, one of the priests who had been at the cathedral for almost fifty years though he had worked there thirty years before he received his calling to serve God as a priest. Unlike Mr Rossovich, Father Poveda answered the phone as if he had been sitting next to it with his hand poised.

It turned out the ageing priest was suffering with insomnia though he elected not to share the root cause. Assured his residence was walking distance and that Mr Rossovich would escort them – probably to make sure they left his house as soon as possible - Anastasia insisted they walk.

Daniel did nothing to hide his lack of interest in that plan, but walk they did, heading back out into the night once more.

Father Poveda welcomed them into his abode despite Mr Rossovich's urgent and obvious hand signals. However, having done so, he paused in the doorway in a Columbo-like manner as if something had just occurred to him.

"Are you able to enter my house?" he asked in accented, but perfect English.

Daniel's eyebrows flickered.

"You're thinking of vampires, old man."

"And I'm a former British Army Officer," Anastasia chipped in. "Hardly evil at all." Though the piece of shrapnel in her head had scrambled her memories, she retained a sense that her former military bosses were mostly incompetent fools. For a second she considered qualifying her comment, but decided it was best to just let it go.

Dismissed, Mr Rossovich turned to leave as swiftly as he could only to find Anastasia had hooked her hand into the crook of his elbow.

"Don't do anything silly like calling the police, okay? If they corner us, it will just end badly for them."

He nodded his head vigorously. "Áno. Žiadna polícia. Rozumiem."

Ana turned her head to check what he had said with Daniel.

The demon was already going through the door, but said, "He got it."

Letting the frightened man go and feeling bad despite herself because he didn't deserve it, Anastasia watched for a second, then followed her demon into the priest's house.

Father Poveda's house was that of a person with limited means and no interest in frivolous things. Sparsely decorated and furnished, the décor was dated, but the house itself was neat and clean.

He led them to a room in the back where he had two tired, wing-back armchairs and an old wooden stool.

He indicated that his guests should take the chairs, but the man was eighty if he was a day and there was no chance Anastasia was going to let him sit on the rickety looking thing. She hurried around him to claim it, smiling generously while angling her arm at the spare chair and noting that Daniel hadn't thought twice about settling himself into the nearest one.

His story was a simple one though it was clear it pained the old man to recall it for them. Unlike with Mr Rossovich, there was no need for Daniel to translate: Father Poveda expressed pleasure at being able to employ his English.

When the shield resulted in multiple deaths before anyone could figure out why there were people lying dead on the ground amidst the rubble, it was Father Poveda who was tasked with securing the artefact safely.

"It was terrifying," he said, his liver spotted hands clasped firmly in his lap. "Everyone who had touched it was dead and the archbishop declared the object – we could only see a small part of it sticking out of the broken column – to be a holy relic. Well, I have to say I doubted that from the start, but it wasn't my place to question his eminence. There were four of us staring at it, all men who worked at the cathedral in one role or another. We needed to call the authorities – we had dead bodies on the ground next to us, but we knew if they came, someone else would touch the shield and the death toll would rise."

Engrossed in his tale, Anastasia found she was leaning forward. "What did you do?"

Father Poveda shifted in his chair, making himself comfortable before continuing.

"We poked at it. Throwing pieces of wood or rock – whatever we had around us, just to see if it was electrified and that was the cause of death. Nothing happened. Eventually, I chose to be brave, held my breath, and prodded it with a length of wood, a broom handle if you can believe that. Everyone else had backed away, but had tied ropes around me so they could yank me back to break my connection with the shield if they needed to. Obviously, nothing happened. We were guessing, but it appeared that so long as we didn't make physical contact with the artefact, we were fine. We used wood, and Henri – he was a verger's apprentice – he ran down to the local carpenter to have a box made. We got the shield free of the rubble and only then could we see what it was. I'm sure you can imagine the conversations that followed. The archbishop insisted it had been hidden for a reason –

God's purpose for it would be revealed when the time was right, and it wasn't for us to question. It was sealed inside the box, none of us touching the shield or the box with our hands, and carried using ropes into a storage room at the back of the cathedral."

Anastasia was fascinated by the history but could wait no longer, "So where is it now?"

Father Poveda smiled, but the expression did not convey humour. It looked more like an apology.

"I'm afraid to say you are too late. I gave it away just a few months ago."

Her brow wrinkled.

"Gave it away? Gave it away to who?" A spasm made her body tense when the obvious answer presented itself. "Was it a demon?" she asked, horrified for what she was about to hear.

However, the old man shook his head.

"A man came one night. I was on my way home and … there were demons, and he was fighting them."

Daniel sat forward in his chair. He'd been bored until that moment, almost nodding off more than once in the comfort and warmth of the old man's house.

"A man was fighting demons? A wizard? Was he German?"

Father Poveda tilted his head, deciphering Daniel's question.

"No. He was a shifter, is that the right word? A werewolf. I would have turned and gone the other way, but ... the red stuff the demons throw around ..."

"Hellfire?" Anastasia supplied.

"Yes. Yes, that's right. I've heard them call it that on TV. I was too close to the fight, I guess. I came around a corner and there it was ahead of me. Before I could do anything, a ball of that hellfire almost took my head off. I ducked and ... well, I'm eighty-three and I fell over and struck my hip on the ground. I couldn't get up and I had to sit there watching it all."

Daniel was still struggling to believe what he was being told.

"A werewolf was fighting demons. Demons. Plural. Not just one but lots and he didn't die instantly?"

Father Poveda shrugged his shoulders.

"Yes. Is that unusual? He was huge; easily half a metre taller than the demons, and he was unbelievably violent. The demons fled, running back to hell, I guess. That's when I saw why he was fighting. There were two young people; a man and a woman in their early twenties. I have to tell you my faith in God was strengthened that night."

Daniel pulled an incredulous face.

"Really? You see demons and werewolves fighting and it strengthens your faith?"

The old priest smiled at his demonic guest.

"Of course. Amongst all the confusion, all the unrest and the general belief that the end of times is fast approaching, there was this man fighting to protect people he didn't know. He was like the hand of God personified. The couple were also werewolves I discovered. The tall one came to check on me, carrying me home and making sure I didn't need medical attention. His name is Zachary."

Daniel went very still. He hadn't connected the dots, but now he knew precisely who the werewolf was and how he'd been able to take the shield.

Anastasia, however, was still in the dark.

"I still don't understand how he now has the shield. That's what you are telling me, right? You gave him the shield. How can he touch it without dying? Shifters are human."

"Because he's immortal," Daniel sighed, closing his eyes, and cupping his brow with both hands.

"Wait. What?" Anastasia looked from the demon to the priest and back again, needing an explanation.

Father Poveda said, "I cannot say whether that is true or not. I believe only God is truly immortal and eternal, yet he assured me the shield would not kill him. He asked me about it, in fact. Not that he knew it was a shield. He said he could feel it calling to him. You will ask why I let him have it, but you already have the answer: what I saw that night was a knight of the Lord. Selflessly, he was waging a war against these demons." He made a point of not looking Daniel's way when he spat the word. "They had become a plague upon our city in recent months, targeting supernaturals, he told me and I believed him."

Anastasia wasn't sure what to think. The shield was in the possession of a shifter; a powerful one who was possibly immortal – she could ask Daniel about that later since he seemed to know something about it. It was far better than Beelzebub having it, so now she just needed to find this Zachary person and convince him to hand it over.

Easy, right?

"Where can I find him?" she asked, reinforcing her question with, "My need for the shield is greater than his. I believe I can kill Beelzebub. Actually, I believe I might be the only person on the face of the earth who can kill Beelzebub. I must have the shield. Is he still here in Mostar?"

The old priest pursed his lips and thought for a moment, weighing up his options and deciding what to do before speaking.

"I do not know where Zachary is or whether he stayed in Mostar. He was here for a time; that is how I came to know him and chose to give him the shield."

"Do you have a phone number for him?" Anastasia was not going to be beaten.

Father Poveda shook his head slowly from side to side.

"I'm afraid not. I'm sorry, but I have no information to give you. It was never mine to possess."

Daniel spoke, interrupting before Anastasia could ask another question.

"The shifters will know where he is. At least, they will have a better idea. If he is here, they will be able to lead us to him."

Chapter 27

With Gana as a tour guide, Zac and the pack found the SIA prisoners in no time at all.

"Mum!" Rocco ran to greet his mother, interlocking fingers with her through the bars. His father was there too, pleased to see his son though he was in a different cage and had to watch from across the room.

They were housed in four large cages on the lowest basement floor of the building. Fitting floor to ceiling, the bars were too strong for even the shifters to break, and so far below ground, the wizards and witches were unable to draw on the ley line energy they needed to conjure magic.

Rocco was far from the only member of the rescue party to find his loved ones; everyone else ran around Zac to seek out their friends, family, and lovers.

With no one he needed to greet or be reunited with, Zachary chose to approach Antonio.

The pack alpha eyed him with a neutral expression.

"I have you to thank for this?" he asked before Zachary reached his cage. To Antonio's left and right, men and women were crying and hugging through the bars.

Instead of answering, Zac extended his hand, "When I get these cages open, you're not going to start another fight, are you?"

Antonio laughed, a huffing sound that shook his shoulders.

"No, I think I learned my lesson." He reached a hand through the bar and slapped it into Zachary's. "Thank you. Is there a way out?"

Turning his head to call to Gana, Zac asked, "Got any shilt locked up in here?"

Gana looked up from the control panel she stood behind. She was trying to decipher the unfamiliar controls to open the cages – they were electronically locked, she knew that much, but was having no luck so far.

"Shilt? Um, not that I know of. Why?"

Zac pulled a face, crossing the room so he could speak with her at a volume no one else would hear.

"Because I was going to use them to open a portal and get everyone out of here."

Gana nodded her head. "That's good thinking. Or it would be if we had any shilt here. I was wondering how you proposed to escape. The way in will be cut off by now, Director Alpi recalled everyone the moment you attacked."

Accentuating her words, a voice boomed over the address system.

"This is Captain Fortuna of the SIA. There are police coming to reinforce us. We wish to discuss a peaceable surrender. There is no need for any further bloodshed. Your ... unique skills are wanted, so we have no desire to hurt anyone."

Gana gritted her teeth. "Fortuna is an idiot. He'll tell you anything he can think up to make you believe he had good intentions and then storm this place."

Had it been Zac alone, he would have chosen to fight just for the fun of it. However, the shifters and other supernaturals in the cell area would suffer if he did, and there would be casualties.

Chapter 28

Extending his second sight allowed Daniel to see the thread of elemental energy stretching from the ley lines beneath the city to the supernaturals connected to it. Years ago, it had been difficult to find the one or maybe two supernaturals hidden in a population. They were so sparse and hard to find, he had relied upon the shilt who crossed between realms to feed at night to locate the potential familiars he needed.

Now, though, they were everywhere, and that brought with it a new challenge – how to find the ones he wanted. In the area he could see, his second sight projecting over a radius of almost a kilometre, there had to be nearly a hundred supernaturals.

Anastasia saw when a grin appeared.

"Found them," Daniel announced confidently.

She flicked her right eyebrow skyward.

"How can you be so sure you have the right ones? Just a moment ago you said there were too many to be able to figure it out."

"Ah, yes, well I was forgetting a simple rule. Elemental magicians are usually solitary. Shifters tend to gather in packs. I have a clump of them not far from here which would be about right given that Father Poveda came across them on his way home."

They had already left the old priest's house and were out in the cool night air again. Anastasia shivered, wishing she had an extra layer.

Wanting to get on with it and hoping it would be a simple task, she took Daniel's hand even though he hadn't offered it.

"Come on then. Let's go."

Anastasia expected Daniel to bounce them through a portal so was surprised when he tugged her hand and set off on foot. Yet more surprising was his choice to keep hold of her hand. Ana stared down at their intertwined digits. Her hand looked tiny in his, the tips of her fingers barely poking out from the edge of his palm.

"What are we doing?" she asked, curiosity driving the words from her mouth, for the demon, while attractive, was far from her ideal mate. Their earlier tryst had been a spur of the moment thing; an idea born in a vulnerable moment.

She had no regrets about it; she initiated it after all, but when Daniel realised what he was doing and dropped her hand without a word or a thought, she hated the disappointment that welled inside her heart.

To be wanted – was it a thing she would ever know?

Without turning to look her way, Daniel said, "It's too close to bother with a portal. We'll be there soon."

Expecting ... actually, Anastasia acknowledged that she really hadn't known what to expect, she couldn't hide the frown that formed when Daniel led her toward an auto tuning shop.

"They're in here?" she questioned because it didn't look residential at all.

"Behind it."

Daniel led her around the back of the low-budget auto place, and through a wide gate in a chain-link fence.

A snort escaped her nose. "Really? Werewolf bikers? Isn't that something of a stereotype? I'm sure I've seen crappy videos from the 90s with this exact theme."

If Daniel had thoughts on the subject, he kept them to himself and said, "We'll know soon enough."

"What are you going to do, just knock on the door?"

Daniel shrugged but didn't break stride as he walked toward a sign that boasted 'Synovia diabla Motorkársky klub'. Anastasia didn't need to be able to read the sign to know what she was looking at. The translation was easy – Son of the Devil Motorcycle Club - and not least for all the chrome and leather adorning the row of parked bikes they were passing.

The club house, if that was the right thing to call it, had a large awning covering a raised wooden deck on which chairs and tables were haphazardly arranged. Ashtrays filled with cigarette butts, empty beer bottles and stained glasses adorned each table as if the former occupants had been beamed up midway through an evening of ruining their bodies.

The building itself was brick, the black roof slate tile, but there was no mistaking that it was a repurposed industrial unit. A high roller door dominated one half of the front façade, set off to the right as they faced it. Daniel made his way to a door with a window to its right.

Filling his hand with hellfire, he asked, "Do you want me to knock? They might not be friendly."

Anastasia shoved him out of the way, grabbing the hellfire orb with her right hand to absorb it.

"They won't be friendly if you blow their door off. Maybe I should knock instead."

She didn't knock, of course. It was the dead of night, and anyone inside would be sleeping. Soundly, if the number of beer bottles littering the seating area was anything to go by.

Hammering on the door with an armour-clad fist, Anastasia shouted, "Hello? Hello, I need to speak to someone about an immortal were-wolf and a magical shield. It's rather important so I'm just going to keep hammering until someone comes to speak with me." She fell silent to listen, then shouted, "Sorry," for good measure.

Turning to give Daniel a beaming smile backed by positive thoughts, she waited. After ten seconds, she lifted her hand to try again and was about to smack the roller door to see if that would make even more noise when a light came on above her head. Not an exterior light, but a light inside the building, that when she looked, showed figures moving about to cast shadows.

"Hello," she called again. "We're quite friendly."

"I'm a demon," Daniel muttered. "I don't do friendly."

"Really quite friendly," she insisted, jabbing an elbow into the demon's side. Hitting him with a forced smile, she said, "Is it too much for me to expect you to play nice for a few minutes?"

Daniel made a big show of copying her winning smile. He looked like a politician, but not in a good way. He might win office just for the million-dollar gleam to his teeth but would be embezzling funds and sleeping with his aides before the votes were counted.

There were voices coming from inside and more lights coming on. None of the voices were aimed at her and though they were in Croatian, it was clear they were arguing.

"What are they saying?"

Daniel tilted his head as he digested the garbled speech coming from inside the clubhouse.

"They appear to be generally upset," he replied calmly. "There is a lot of swearing, mostly at each other. The good news is that they are the right bunch; I heard more than one of them mention Zachary."

Taking hold of Daniel's jacket, Ana backed away a metre from the door just as the lights on the ground floor came on.

The sound of someone unlocking the door they faced was accompanied by an electronic whir and then the sound of the roller door rising.

Ana felt as much and saw Daniel draw in source energy to form hellfire orbs and elbowed him yet again.

"No, Daniel," she scowled. "There's no reason for them to not help me. Let's not give them one."

The shifters burst from the building in a line, three leaving via the door one after the other to fan out while two dozen more men and women stepped out from under the rising roller door before it was past waist high.

As one they straightened. Most were only half dressed; their shirts deemed unnecessary, and many hadn't bothered with footwear.

Anastasia's interaction with shifters was almost nil, so she didn't see the threat for what it was – they didn't bother with clothes because they planned to shift. In their werewolf forms they were significantly more dangerous and far harder to hurt.

Daniel knew it though and had moved away from Anastasia to get a clear line of sight for when he needed to start throwing hellfire around.

Anastasia waved and said, "Hello," before anyone else got a chance to speak. She smiled brightly at the same time. "I'm Anastasia."

A ripple went along the line though truly it started in multiple places. The shifters were looking at each other, confirming what they already knew to be true: this was the woman they'd seen on TV.

Anastasia was looking for a leader, hooking an eyebrow as she waited for someone to respond.

"They know who you are," quipped Daniel. "You want to do autographs and selfies or get to the point?"

Ignoring her impulse to stick a sinfire orb up Daniel's butt, Anastasia maintained her friendly attitude.

"I really need to find Zachary. Can you help me? Daniel, can you translate, please?"

Daniel opened his mouth but was saved the effort.

"What do you want with Zachary?" asked a woman. She was one of the three who came out through the main door and thus was nearest to Anastasia. That wasn't why she spoke though, Ana assessed.

She was the alpha.

Dressed in denim jeans, a simple white tee that betrayed the lack of bra beneath, and a black leather waistcoat displaying the club colours, she was in her forties and heavy around the hips. Neither her age nor her waist size diminished her confidence. The men and women around her saw her as dominant.

Anastasia met the woman's guarded eyes with a smile.

"I need to talk to him about the shield. You know which one I am talking about, right?" To make it all very clear, she thought of her own armour; the simple act that always made it come to life above her skin.

Most of the shifters had not been looking her way. Despite the fact that Daniel hadn't spoken yet, the werewolves were watching him warily like they could tell what he was.

"You have seen me on TV," Ana tried to anticipate their thoughts, "but what you have heard is not true. The battle with the demons is coming, and I might be the only one who can stop them." To further accentuate her point, she sent source energy down her arms to form hellfire.

It got the shifters' attention, and caused half their number to react by transforming.

Ana shouted, "I am not a demon!" as she let the hellfire orbs reabsorb into the palms of her hands. "I am human. So far as I know. I am the only human on earth who can do what I can do, and this sword," she jerked her head to the pommel and grip as they extended past her right shoulder, "can kill the demons."

"You're lying," spat the alpha, her eyes travelling away from Anastasia to lock on Daniel, "and that's a demon."

Automatically, the line of shifters tensed like players waiting for the referee to start the game. Those who had not yet transformed did so, their skin darkening and hardening as they prepared for their alpha to release them. Of the entire pack, only she stayed in human form.

Anastasia begged, "Wait!" but she did so just as Daniel formed hellfire – a defensive reaction only held in check in deference to Anastasia's wishes.

The sight of the fizzing, dark red orbs and the confirmation of Daniel's heritage acted as a trigger. The shifters leapt.

Chapter 29

D eep in the basement beneath the SIA headquarters in Rome, Zachary faced an unexpected issue.

"Damned shifters! This is your fault! You're the menace they want off the streets!" The ill-advised words came from a barrel-bellied man with a scruffy beard. The last of the cells had been opened, the door clanging back against its stops as the man burst through it.

Antonio's pack twisted to face him as one, many of them tugging at their clothes as they started to transform.

The wizard was being held back by other elemental magicians from the same cell, but it wasn't because they disagreed with his statement. Down here beneath the ley lines, the wizards were powerless. The shifters, who could transform at will – their magic working differently, were just as deadly as ever.

Antonio chose to calm the situation.

"My friend, we did not cause this. Director Alpi said we were needed to help them fight against the impending demon threat, but we are as in the dark about why we were taken as you are."

The opinionated wizard saw the statement as fuel for his fire.

"That's utter rubbish. You lot were fighting in the streets! It was all over the internet. I even recognise him!" the wizard jabbed an accusing hand at Zachary. "The SIA had to react. You forced their hand."

"Ah, that's not entirely true." The comment came from Gana, and it silenced everyone in the room.

Wanting to hear more, Zac asked, "What do you mean? Why did the SIA raid Rome tonight? Are they building an army?"

Gana failed to hide the grimace crossing her face when she said, "Well, yes, they are. The order to grab supernaturals by force came from Ironbolt himself." She didn't need to explain to anyone who President Colt Ironbolt was; the world knew his face. "I'm not sure what happened elsewhere around the world, but here Alpi believed it was the right thing to do. The world probably does need an army of supernaturals, but this is not the way to do it."

"How can you say that?" raged the angry wizard, his voice backed this time by several others. "You work for him! You're part of this!"

"I am helping to defend the people of the world, Rodrigo", Gana argued her case. "And I came here to rescue you all because what happened tonight was so wrong."

"Attention. Attention. This is Captain Fortuna. If you do not surrender, I will be forced to employ tear gas to subdue you." The voice from the address system echoed slightly in the confined space, the sound fading away as whispers replaced it.

The angry wizard might have been interrupted, but he wasn't done.

"You're a traitor!" he snapped at Gana. "You think you can do what you want because you are more powerful? Yes, I know who you are, Gana. The returned familiars are few enough that the rest of us know who you are. You may be powerful on the surface, but down here you're not."

Dismissing his beef with the werewolves because he couldn't do anything about them, Rodrigo, the angry wizard, started across the room on an intercept course.

Gana's eyes flared in shock. Having willingly descended past the point where she could perform magic, she was nothing more than a hundred- and twenty-pound African woman. The angry wizard and his friends could hurt her and there would be nothing she could do to stop them.

Zachary took two steps and swung his left hand to deliver a backhanded slap to Rodrigo's face. The blow sounded like a cow's carcass hitting a butcher's block and though it was delivered with a fraction of the effort he could have employed, it felled Rodrigo instantly.

"That's enough." Zachary's statement wasn't shouted. He didn't growl or snarl. Yet the two words were enough to halt the advancing tide of elemental magicians and silence everyone in the room. "Now. A rescue isn't much of a rescue until everyone successfully escapes. I expected to find shilt here and to be able to use them to create a portal. Gana assures me there are none. That means we need to fight our way out. I am going first. The bottleneck of the stairs will work in our favour." His remark made a few eyebrows twitch in question, so he explained, "The shield will deflect whatever weapons they try to employ, and they will not be able to get around it to hit anyone else."

"What about the tear gas?" asked Rocco.

Zachary acknowledged his point.

"We have little choice but to push through it."

Once again, it was Gana who changed his plans. "There is another way we can do this."

Chapter 30

Reacting with a grunt of effort, Anastasia threw up her arms. With source energy that surged from her core, drawn from the earth by her will, she launched a sustained stream of hellfire. Unable to select sinfire whenever she had absorbed its deadlier opposite, she cursed that she had taken some from Daniel. It was habit now, and one she knew she would continue because hellfire was so much more potent.

However, its deadly nature dictated that she could not use it on the shifters, so her aim was not at them but at Daniel. Striking him with a sustained stream that tore his feet from the ground and flung him twenty metres, her intention was twofold: stop him from killing anyone and exhaust her supply of hellfire.

The chain link fence fought to stay in one piece when the demon struck it, but by then Anastasia was only half watching. The moment her hellfire stuttered and lightened, replaced by the sinfire her body naturally produced, she shifted her aim.

To her left, the alpha was yelling something. It went unheard by everyone. The shifters were too focussed on addressing the threat, and Anastasia could hear nothing above the rush of blood to her head and the shouts coming from the werewolves.

They were turning her way, undeterred by her display of power, so she hit them. Sweeping them from their feet like pins before a bowling ball, they tumbled and collided.

A twitch of her left hand took out the two who exited the building alongside the alpha and as she let the stream of pure, light-blue energy dwindle and die, only Ana and the alpha were standing.

With a shake of her head to get her hair to shift away from her eyes, Anastasia restated her position.

"I need to speak to Zachary."

Swearing and cursing, Daniel was getting to his feet.

"Anastasia, I swear I will cut off your hair while you sleep if you ever do that again! You think you have scars now! I will take your prosthetics …"

"Oh, shut up, Daniel! One simple rule: don't kill people. It's not exactly hard to follow."

The demon was spitting mad and looked like he was going to create fresh hellfire. Anastasia stood her ground, facing the alpha, but looking Daniel's way.

He was mad, but that was better than letting him kill members of the pack.

Cautiously optimistic that Daniel wasn't going to retaliate, Ana tried to settle things before the pack was back on its collective feet.

They were already getting up when she asked, "Can we do this peacefully?"

The alpha, a woman called Marija Frajt, knew she was beaten. Her pack had lost members to demons before, hence their desire to deliver the first blow, but she'd seen nothing like the display the tiny woman with the scarred face had just put on. Whatever she was, Anastasia Aaronson's claim to be the only one in the world capable of defeating the demons had a ring of truth to it – Marija had just seen her put one down.

With her pack members bouncing back to their feet as they recovered, and moments from resuming their attack, she spoke aloud, "Enough."

"Enough?" questioned her beta, a tough man she'd once been fool enough to let into her bed. Until that point, he'd been content to let her lead, but sleeping with him had somehow changed the relationship dynamics and she'd been remiss in addressing it. "He's a demon and she's wanted by every law enforcement organisation on the planet, Marija!"

"And she just beat you like a child with a toy, Goran. Would you like her to do it again?"

Goran was too riled to see sense.

"So what? You're proposing to invite her in? To give her what she wants?" he demanded in a derisory tone. "Why don't you let the demon in too, Marija? Perhaps he would like to take some of the packs' children."

"Are they shifters?" asked Daniel, sounding interested and not helping matters.

Meeting Anastasia's eyes, Marija said, "No. The demon stays outside." It was a challenge; a statement that Ana could accept or choose to fight.

With a nod, Anastasia accepted the alpha's terms.

"Can you help me to find Zachary?" Ana had been hoping the man she wanted was here, but that he hadn't appeared seemed indication enough that he most likely wasn't. That proved to be the case, Marija revealed, leading the world's most wanted supernatural terrorist into her club house.

"He left here more than a week ago, following a lead."

Anastasia wasn't sure she'd heard right. "A lead? A lead to what? Is he looking for more pieces of armour?"

Marija didn't answer, making her guest wait while she thumbed a Marlboro from a battered pack and lit it. Blowing ugly blue smoke into the air, she shook her head.

"No, he's looking for someone. A demon. He never did say why, but it was why he came here. He stays a while then ventures off when he hears about another hotbed of demon activity."

"And the demons cannot kill him?" Ana sought to confirm what she still struggled to believe.

"Seen it with my own eyes." Marija took another deep lungful of smoke. "He just turned up here one night looking to pick a fight with some demons. He saved my daughter and her boyfriend. They're both outside now recovering from that little display of yours," the pack alpha said pointedly. "What are you exactly?"

If Marija hoped to strike a nerve by reminding Ana she'd just pummelled almost the entire pack, she was to be disappointed – Ana cared not what she had to do to reach her goal. She would stop short of killing people, but already questioned if that would stay true all the way to the end.

To answer the question, Anastasia gave a truthful response.

"I don't know. I'm not sure anyone does. I'm not a shifter though and I can't conjure magic. Whatever I am, it appears to be the case that I am the only one. Now, are you going to tell me where I can find Zachary, or must I convince you?"

She didn't intend for her question to sound like a threat, but that was how Marija perceived it.

Eyeing the tiny British woman suspiciously, she reached into her back pocket and took out her phone.

Chapter 31

Almost five hundred kilometres away, Zachary's phone rang. However, he was heading up the stairs already and chose to ignore it.

The question in his head had nothing to do with who might be calling him; he was questioning how many floors they could ascend before they met resistance. They needed to climb two floors – four flights of stairs. There, Gana assured them she would be able to tap into the nearest ley line.

It was a weak one but all she needed was enough juice to open a portal. That she had a shilt glove, gifted to her by Otto Schneider himself not more than a week ago, was a secret she'd been keeping from everyone. Truthfully, she didn't want to use it and knew Alpi and others in her SIA detachment would want her to.

To get from one place to another using magic was a powerful tool, but it also involved returning to the demon realm and she'd sworn to herself she would die first. That had been based on the concept that a demon was recapturing her, but the thought of voluntarily returning, even if it was just for a second, made her feel sick.

The pack wanted to return home, but they put up no argument when she pointed out the SIA would just come for them again. The elemental magicians agreed but were unwilling to go wherever the pack were going. They each had other ideas about where they were going to go in contrast to the pack who were united in joining Zac when he suggested Croatia.

He knew of another pack, somewhere they could take refuge for a short time at least.

Advancing up the stairs, Zac's phone rang off and then started again. It gave away his position the first moment it made a noise, though Zac was certain the SIA agents and whoever else was above them would know they were coming anyway.

The pop and fizzing noise of a tear gas canister being fired and falling through the air prompted a charge that Zac led with a roar.

He was right that he could use the shield to protect himself and those behind him from harm but against the tear gas there was little he could do.

Or was there?

Coughing and choking broke out behind him as he raced, bellowing upward through the stairwell. Taking the steps three at a time, he was leaving everyone behind. Cries to 'fall back' reached his ears and he paused, debating if it was members of Antonio's pack he could hear, or the wizards instead.

Even in the darkness of the unlit stairwell, he could see the smoke beginning to fill the void at the bottom. It was rising, but doing their best to stay above it, TJ, Rocco, Joshua, and more ran. Antonio and his wife were there and driven ahead of them, the woman they needed above all others – Gana.

Her left hand was gloved now, ready for the conjuring that would open a portal and deliver them to safety.

Another pop and fizz – a salvo of them, in fact, as the SIA agents led by Captain Fortuna sent a fresh wave of tear gas down the stairs. This time, Zachary was waiting.

With his left arm extended into the gap the stairs wrapped around, he caught two of the canisters. Both were spewing thick, evil poison, and he sent each of them flying back up from whence they came.

His immortality; the magic that had caused it and now repaired his body each time it was hurt, failed to react swiftly enough to prevent the tear gas tearing at his lungs. Zachary, heaving for air and fighting against effects that caught him by surprise, pushed himself to continue his ascent. Running to get to the next landing and expecting to encounter new countermeasures from the SIA at any moment, his feet faltered when he heard Gana's yell.

"I have a ley line!" she managed to shout between gagging coughs.

"Me too!" yelled another wizard, one of only three who chose to come with the shifters.

Maintaining his focus on the SIA high above them, Zac shouted back, "Can you open a portal?"

"Yes, but I don't know where I am going!"

Backing up, Zac reversed down the stairs, gathering straggling members of the pack as he ushered them back toward Gana.

Captain Fortuna and the SIA were reacting to his question – they'd heard it, and feared the supernaturals they'd captured earlier were about to escape. The sound of their boots, fast on the stairs, gave additional urgency to their situation.

Finding Gana in the dark, the witch hiding her face inside the cloth of her dress to minimise the tear gas exposure, Zac grabbed her arm and yelled, "Just get us out of here!" Zac did his best to speak without breathing; he could refill his lungs once they were away from the tear gas. Around him, everyone was fighting the awful effects and they were losing. "Take us to the demon realm and then to anywhere in Croatia. Can you do that?"

Gana didn't answer. She didn't want to say anything; doing so would mean exposing the sensitive soft tissue of her mouth to the searing, stinging gas. She also didn't want to open a portal. It was all her idea; she suggested it, but now that the time was upon her, she was gripped by fear.

The SIA would reprimand her for helping the escaping supers, but they wouldn't fire her. She was a rescued familiar and cherished above almost all the supernaturals in the mortal realm.

Choosing to surrender instead, she moved to back away, but Zac was still holding her arm.

"I can't do it!" she cried, coughing instantly when the toxic gas filled her lungs.

"Yes, you can! Gana, you have the power to transport everyone to safety. Do it now!"

"No, I ..." Her reply was cut off by the arrival of the SIA.

The agents were in uniform, dark and hard to make out by design, but the dim light in the stairwell reflected off the lenses of their respirators, and they carried weapons that used laser targeting, the thin red beams cutting through the smoke to highlight the agents' locations.

Deploying stun guns – weapons deploying an electric shock to over-whelm a person's nervous system, the SIA advanced.

To Zac's left and right, pack members twitched, spasmed, and fell. Electrodes hit his back too, but the magic maintaining his immortality fought against the electricity raging through his body, allowing him to largely ignore it.

Gana's eyes were wide with fear and shock, and she gawped open-mouthed at the still twitching bodies by her feet even as she coughed and wretched. Were Zachary not holding her arm, she would have hugged the ground, but his bulk had protected her from being hit and he left her with little choice but to comply when he lifted her from the ground.

"Open a portal, Gana. Do it now or I will deal with the SIA agents and then make you open one."

Terrified beyond the ability to think, Gana reached out with her left hand.

Chapter 32

M arija had just about given up trying to contact Zac by phone. It was the middle of the night in Mostar, and if Zac was still in Rome, then the time there was little different. He was asleep or with a woman, or in the middle of a fight knowing Zac.

Hell, maybe he'd finally caught up to Rebecca and he was doing something unspeakable. He'd never really talked about it; that wasn't Zac's style, but Marija was nevertheless left with the impression that a volcano simmered deep beneath the surface, waiting to erupt if he ever came face to face with the demon he sought.

Grimacing at her phone, conscious Anastasia's eyes were on her, Marija was wondering if the British woman would accept the need to wait until dawn when the sound of something happening outside reached her ears.

Anastasia heard it too. Her first thought was that Daniel had quietly woven an elemental spell to subdue the shifters despite her demands to leave them be. He didn't like to be threatened and his history of dominance over mankind caused him to act irrationally on an hourly basis.

Both women hurried to the door. They had not gone far past the lobby, just into a side room, but bumping against each other in their haste to get outside again, they heard anguished cries that sped their feet.

Expecting to find Marija's pack fighting against whatever conjuring Daniel had dreamt up, Ana was shocked to find the scene outside was anything but what she imagined.

A portal was just closing and stumbling away from it were at least three dozen people. They were coughing and choking and a cloud of … mist or dust surrounded and coated them. That they were shifters was never in question – half the number were still transformed.

They couldn't all be shifters though because someone had opened the portal. Ana's first reaction was to ready sinfire, though her fingers twitched to grab for the sword on her back.

Marija's pack were moving toward the newcomers, hesitantly for the most part but seeing young people – teenagers – and all of them suffering, more were overcoming their initial caution.

The wind shifted, bringing with it the tang of CS gas, a smell Ana knew only too well from her training days in the Army. It made her skin prickle, and her breath catch even from the miniscule dose the breeze delivered.

She thought about calling a warning, telling Marija's pack to 'hold back', but what was she seeing? Was there a demon? Was there danger? Had they somehow tracked her and Daniel?

Shooting her head around to find her companion, she breathed a small sigh of relief to find him sitting on the bonnet of a Mercedes car just beyond the pack's compound. She also saw when he stiffened and tracked his wide eyes to find two figures coming through the portal just as it shut.

Anastasia had never met or even heard of Zachary Barnabus. Hell, she didn't even know his last name, but the description of the immortal werewolf would have been enough to convince her the seven-foot-tall form she was now looking at was the man she wanted. He was enormously muscular, his bare arms and legs looking like they could have been chiselled from granite. The dark, almost ebony black hue to his skin only added to the comparison, but no guesswork was needed to tell her she had found the man who held the shield she needed.

Because he was holding it.

Hope blossomed in her chest. Relief too for the task of locating the shield had been relatively simple.

Starting toward him and ignoring the sting of tear gas coming from those she approached, Ana watched as he flexed his arm and the shield withdrew, becoming less visible and vanishing just as her armour did each time she chose to hide it.

"Zachary?" she called, unsure what she ought to say and how the giant werewolf might react to her imminent demand. There was no reason she could see to greet him with anything other than a pleasant smile, and when he looked up to find who had called his name, she did just that.

"I know you?" he asked, dividing his attention between Ana and a tall, thin African woman he held by one arm as if she was a captured prize.

Ana's initial assessment that the woman was being held against her will disappeared when she watched Zachary hoist her into his arms.

Marija's pack knew fellow shifters when they saw them and Zac's arrival with them eroded any final caution being employed.

Marija's instruction to, "Help them. Get them inside," spurred her pack members on. Zachary strode through them, the magic inside him fighting against the ill-effects of the tear gas to leave him looking unaffected.

He was carrying the African woman, her weight insignificant in his arms, and making for the club house with no intention of stopping to talk to Anastasia.

Left with the option of helping the new arrivals – they needed it – or obstructing his path so she could get to the task in hand, Ana chose to muck in with everyone else. Zac was clearly intent on getting the choking shifters inside the building, so lending a hand was the right thing to do if she wanted to ingratiate herself.

However, before she could get to the nearest shifter, a woman who had already transformed back to human form, Anastasia saw Zachary freeze.

He'd spotted Daniel.

Chapter 33

I n typical Daniel fashion, he'd chosen to stay in plain sight when he ought to have hidden. Zachary would react badly; he knew that, yet instead of opening a portal and slipping away or simply stepping into the shadows, he'd chosen to remain where he was sitting on the bonnet of the car.

Ana had her arms out to help a poor woman whose eyes were so red and swollen from the effects of the tear gas that it was clear she could barely see. With a muttered apology, she dismissed her.

Zac was lowering the African woman to the ground, doing so carefully, but also with haste.

"Zachary," Ana called out as she wove through both packs of shifters, one helping the other and all heading for the clubhouse. "Zachary, please. I need to talk to you. It's about the shield." Should she say that Daniel was with her? The demon had done something to anger the werewolf which came as no surprise. He hadn't said what it was and that was as expected too. But would Zachary help her ... give her the shield if he knew she was with the demon?

Surely, she wouldn't be able to hide that fact from the shifter anyway.

It was too late though. Daniel had seen the werewolf, and though he might have fled in uncontrolled panic when the horsemen showed up in Louisiana, he wasn't about to show fear to a human.

Zachary handed the African woman over to two women from Marija's pack, murmuring something as he stood once more.

He was being cautious; keeping his rage in check for he knew the humans around him would serve as easy targets for the demon if he started throwing hellfire.

Daniel moved away from the car, drawing source energy through his body. The power he channelled cracked over his skin and down his arms, tiny sparks like static electricity appeared above the surface of his clothing - a deliberate threat display. He knew Zachary was supposedly immortal, but just like Otto Schneider, he saw it as a challenge. Maybe the werewolf could survive hellfire, but how much could he take before he was unable to get up?

Daniel was prepared to find out. He would beat the werewolf into submission or unconsciousness and then Anastasia could take the shield. That ought to speed things up.

Gasps and cries echoed across the forecourt of the clubhouse as the shifters ran, Marija's pack helping the newcomers from Rome to hurry them out of harm's way. But not all of them ran for cover.

Some stayed.

Antonio for one chose to face off against the demon and because he stayed, so too did others from his pack.

Zachary shook his head. "This is my fight."

"And we will fight alongside you," Antonio replied without needing a beat to think.

It was understood – they felt they owed Zachary a debt and maybe they did. He'd rescued them from the SIA and saved Rocco from the demons before that, but that was the point really. Why do any of it if he was just going to let them die now?

He shook his head again. "No. This I must do alone."

Coming to stand in his way, Anastasia held her arms out to show she carried no weapons in them.

"You don't have to do it at all. I have no doubt you want to kill Daniel, goodness knows I do half the time, but the threat the world faces is bigger than that."

Zachary cast his eyes down. "You sound like the SIA. That's the same lie they keep trying to sell."

"It's not a lie. We must work together."

"Is that what you've been doing? Is it, Anastasia Aaronson," Zac named the diminutive woman standing between him and the demon.

"Is that why you are the most wanted person on Earth? Stand aside. I will go through you if I must."

Anastasia was starting to think the same thing; she could strike now. She could kill him and take the shield if he refused to yield, but in a decision she genuinely wasn't sure about, she chose to let the fight happen.

Daniel probably had it coming after all, and in a battle of demon versus werewolf, her money was going with the demon every time.

Stepping to one side, she spoke to the gaggle of shifters flanking Zachary.

"You should do as he says and sit this one out. No one needs to die tonight."

With a nod of confirmation from Zac, Antonio and his pack members backed away, but no one was going very far – they wanted to watch. Rocco was whispering urgently, telling those close enough to hear all about what he'd seen Zac do back in Rome.

Anastasia looked at Daniel, but the demon didn't meet her eyes. With a shrug of acceptance, she got out of the way too.

She walked to the far end of the courtyard, back to the corner of the auto repair place where she felt confident she could still react if there was cause to.

The giant werewolf wasn't doing anything; he was just standing there facing his opponent. Not that it was a mystery why – he was giving the mortals a chance to get to cover.

The moment he considered it safe, Zachary leapt. To Anastasia's eyes, the sudden shift from motionless was a blur. She expected Daniel to smash the werewolf from the air with repeated hits of hellfire and was surprised when she saw him conjuring elemental magic.

Daniel had chosen to do what he believed his opponent would not expect. Demons always use hellfire, everyone knows that. So he used a basic air spell to swat Zac to one side. Unable to resist it, the werewolf tumbled, but not for long. The talons on his right hand dug into the concrete, arresting his motion in an instant.

Daniel hit him with fire, a gout of white-hot flame blasting the shifter and searing everyone's eyes which is why no one saw the spell miss completely.

Zac knew something was coming. He'd watched Otto Schneider fight and understood what was possible. In truth, he'd been expecting lightning or perhaps the asphyxiation spell they loved so much. He was tensed to react and in the instant before the flame engulfed him, he went vertical.

Reaching a height of over three metres, he came back to earth not on top of Daniel, but several metres to his right whereupon he swung a mighty arm to fell a signpost.

Daniel caught a sense of the projectile before it hit him, but could do nothing to stop the violent impact that slammed his whole body sideways.

The strike got an excited 'Ooooh!" from the crowd of onlookers – members of both packs hanging out of the clubhouse to watch Zac fight.

There was no question whose side they were on.

Following his advantage, Zac crossed the courtyard so fast it was almost impossible to track him, yet he wasn't fast enough.

To buy time, and gasping for breath from the severe injury to his chest, Daniel used hellfire. Pulse after pulse hit the advancing werewolf, slowing and then stopping him. It was a stalling tactic at best, but enough direct strikes would put anything down.

Zachary absorbed the blows, each of them triggering his nerve endings like never-ending electric shocks raging through his body. Leaning into them as if they were a gale trying to sweep him from his feet, he was determined to withstand the torment. He was going to keep moving forward, a centimetre at a time if he had to, closing the gap between them until he could skewer the demon's head.

Seeing his strategy fail, Daniel changed it, loosing his next shots not at Zachary but beyond him to the club house where startled screams and yells made the werewolf look.

Had Gana and the two other wizards not formed barrier shields to hide behind, the hellfire shots might have killed half a dozen of the onlookers.

It was no longer a spectator sport.

Anastasia, seeing the *almost* murder of innocents, pushed off the wall. She was going to end it, taking both parties out of the equation. She didn't get the chance.

Zac spun away from Daniel's next spell, closing the gap again just as the demon manipulated a conjuring of water. He was targeting Zac's body, intending to explode the werewolf from within just as Otto Schneider had with Teague when he and the werewolf gained their immortality.

He only needed a couple of seconds to maintain the spell. Once he was able to weave it sufficiently through Zac's body, there would be nothing the werewolf could do. He might recover, but Teague had never been the same since.

The shifter slowed, struggling against the magic wreaking havoc inside his body.

Sneering, Daniel said, "Walk away from this," and pushed yet more effort into the spell.

One more second, that was all he needed. The werewolf was on his knees now, fighting but losing. Daniel closed in, aiming to stand over the remains of the shifter when the battle was done.

Zac's vision was blurry, but he could see well enough what was in front of his nose. Punching down hard on a manhole cover by his feet, he shattered the concrete that held it in place and the heavy steel plate flipped up. In a single motion, he gripped its edge and threw the thirty-kilo disc of steel at his opponent.

There wasn't a damned thing Daniel could do.

It weighed too much, was going altogether too fast, and the short distance it needed to fly meant it was already too late by the time he saw it.

Anastasia choked, gasping for breath when she saw Daniel's headless body topple backward. She'd never seen anything like it. With the exception of Otto Schneider, she had never seen any human stand up to a demon. It wasn't possible under normal circumstances to inflict enough damage to hurt them. Otto had managed to catch them with a spell that froze them, but it didn't last long.

The werewolf, however, had gone toe to toe and won. Only Daniel's immortality would save him.

Shocked, she took a step forward. Now was the time to capitalise on his injuries. Zac was hurt and she had the weapons she needed to make him give up the shield. Should she employ them though? What did it make her if she did? Maybe he would see sense and hand the shield over if she only asked.

Zac was getting up. He hurt just about everywhere and though he did his best to hide it, he was sure people could see how close he'd come to losing. His brain felt like it was on fire and his heart, which barely sped up when he fought, was going so fast he worried it might stop. Or burst.

Whooping and cheering, both packs of shifters, united by their similarities, came running to congratulate Zac.

He got to his feet, straightening to his full height but never taking his eyes off the demon. Sparkling magical light danced around Daniel's body – the death curse healing him as Zac knew it would.

"Get wood," he wheezed, refusing to clutch his heart though he desperately wanted to. "We can keep him in the healing state indefinitely with a fire. Now that he's down, we have a small window to keep him there."

"No!" Anastasia stepped into their path, protecting Daniel's headless body with her own. "He's been tortured half insane by Beelzebub for helping me to escape. I know you want to hurt him, but he's fighting for us now."

"Bullshit!" Zachary spat the word with venom. "Demons fight for themselves. Maybe he is helping you, but you're blind if you think his aim is altruistic."

He made a fair point and Anastasia knew it; she often wondered what Daniel would do if the death curse fell. Would he stick by her side when the demon horde invaded? Would he chance it all and hope that she could prevail? It was doubtful at best.

Nevertheless, she was standing her ground.

Chapter 34

Staring up at the giant werewolf, Anastasia knew it was decision time. Either he was going to give her the shield or she was going to take it. There was no third option. On top of that, she needed Daniel to help her move around the planet. Without him, she would be caught by the authorities and her quest to find the remaining pieces of armour would get significantly more difficult.

Plus, in the fight that would inevitably ensue when the authorities cornered her, there was a chance she would kill humans and that would make her precisely what they said she was.

"I need that shield," she stated unambiguously.

Her stance and attitude made Zachary laugh.

"Really? What makes you think I might be willing to give it up?" Turning his head slightly to speak to the shifters to his right, he acted as if the tiny British woman were of no concern when he said, "Wood. Anything that will burn. Quickly. And get his body. If we dismember it, we'll have a little more time to play with."

Anastasia whipped her right arm upward, reaching for the God Sword and thrust out her left hand as it filled with sinfire. Source energy coursed through her body, the light blue glow from it startling many of those standing before her.

Not Zachary though. He refused to flinch, glaring down at Anastasia as if daring her to test his patience.

She held the orb of sinfire, ready to send it, but prepared to give diplomacy one last shot. With her right hand gripping the sword – a weapon that could kill Zachary though she doubted he knew it – she held her stance.

"I don't want to fight you ..."

"I wouldn't want to fight me either," Zachary smirked.

"But I have killed dozens of demons." She paused to let her statement sink in. "And I can kill you." With a thought, she brought her armour to life. "I need your shield. Need it. I am not asking for myself, but for humanity." Zachary raised one eyebrow and crossed his arms as he continued to listen. "This is not about me, but I appear to be the only person on earth who can wield this sword. That makes me the only person who can stop Beelzebub when he comes. You might be able to fight a single demon, or maybe even a few, but have you any idea how powerful Beelzebub is?"

Zachary grinned. "I fought him in Bremen a while back. I wasn't all that impressed."

It wasn't a response Anastasia could have anticipated and she got no sense that he was lying. It changed nothing though. He wasn't going to give her the shield no matter what she said.

"This would be easier if you would give it to me willingly. I cannot allow you to keep it." She said the words – a final warning and she already felt regret that she was probably going to have to kill him to obtain that which she had to have, but while speaking, she was assessing his stance, determining how to attack.

Feign and strike? Hit him with sinfire first? Sweep the blade as he came for her and remove an arm? Would that do it?

Zachary hit her.

Maybe she was telling him the truth and her intentions were genuine, but he couldn't know one way or the other. She was clearly missing a hand, the left side of her face was a network of scars ... was she even up to the job she claimed as hers? He doubted it. The shield was a tool he'd never expected, yet it was one he would not now do without.

It was a backhanded slap, lightning fast as he unfolded one arm at a downward angle to hit the woman's side rather than her head. He didn't wish her dead, but she wasn't getting his shield. Once unconscious, they would tie her up and quiz a little more deeply.

The SIA wanted her ... badly. They wanted her badly, but Zachary wasn't about to help them either. He had his people, not that he was part of a pack, but they saw him as an ally and that suited him. He could come and go as he pleased and until he found Rebecca and made her pay for her crimes, he would do just that.

Anastasia almost didn't see the blow coming at all the werewolf moved so fast, and even though she did, there was nothing she could do to stop it. Zachary's arm struck her high on the meaty part of her left shoulder. The sinfire orb formed in her left hand discharged into the ground by her feet as she was knocked from them.

Without the suit of armour to protect her, that one strike might have been all it took, and it didn't help that she weighed a hundred pounds on a good day. Flung sideways, there was nothing she could do to stop herself until she came back to earth. Her right hip bit into the concrete, jarring her, but the suit of armour, even though there were still parts missing, did its job.

She bounced, stuck out her right hand to arrest her motion and with a roll came back to her feet.

Zachary had already turned away, which is why he caught her sustained blast of sinfire in his back.

Like turning on a water cannon, the beam of pure source energy blasted the giant werewolf across the courtyard. Around him members of both packs were caught in the surplus where Ana tried to keep her aim true but inevitably missed when her target tumbled and rolled.

That Zac hadn't expected it was an understatement.

Only when Zachary hit the wall of the auto repair place and went through it did Anastasia release her stream of energy. As the light from it died, gasps of fear and cries of terror were followed by squeals of relief when the shifters outside the blast range saw their fallen colleagues were still alive. Though Marija's pack had witnessed Anastasia's neat trick, most had never seen sinfire before and assumed it would kill just like hellfire.

Zachary was down. He felt like he'd been hit by a truck. Demons had belted him with multiple shots of hellfire on many occasions. It hurt like hell, but he was always able to shake it off and continue fighting. This time, he tried to get his feet back under his body, only to find they didn't quite seem to want to do as he asked.

Anastasia stalked toward him. She could taste blood in her mouth, the result of his back-handed blow. Her ears were ringing, and the stump of her left leg had taken a knock and was pure agony.

She wasn't going to let any of that show.

She wanted to give the werewolf another chance to be reasonable. It wasn't in her nature to kill him, or to chop a piece off just to get his attention, but as she closed on him, walking not running due to the pain in her stump, she saw it was already too late.

The werewolf was getting up.

Commanding sinfire back into her left hand, she fired a sustained stream right at his head.

And missed.

Demon magic needed only a few seconds to repair the damage wrought by Anastasia's sinfire, and almost fully recovered, Zac leapt, aiming straight up to avoid more of the same. Looking down, he saw his timing could not have been better – the sudden flare of bright light from her sinfire had hidden his trajectory and now she was looking around for him.

Sailing through the air, he saw shifters from both packs surging toward her. Transformed into werewolves, they were coming to his aid. It was more than Anastasia could defend against.

Or so Zachary thought.

With a sweep of her arm, the tiny woman felled more than two dozen of the werewolves while they were still five metres from her. The beam of sinfire coming from her outstretched palm was unlike anything Zachary had ever seen.

When she challenged him, his plan was only to prevent her from hurting anyone. Now, he accepted that he was probably going to have to kill her. Whoever she was, whether the news reports about her were true, she was powerful and dangerous and right in his face.

If she wouldn't stop, he knew he would have no choice.

Having travelled right over her head in a looping arc that carried him almost six metres, Zachary landed facing her.

Seeing him, Anastasia threw all her sinfire in his direction, but he knew better than to be casual about the threat she posed now and was ready.

The shield caught the full blast of pure source energy, absorbing it like water into a sponge. Neither Zac nor Ana knew it, but she was just making his defence stronger.

The fight had started less than thirty seconds ago, but that was all the time it took to make the courtyard outside Marija's club house look like a war zone.

Without the benefit of the demon magic coursing through Zachary, those Anastasia knocked down with a lengthy burst of sinfire were not about to get up. They would recover, but for now their bodies were ruined vessels unable to do much more than claw their way across the rough ground to find some cover.

Unnoticed by most, some of the sinfire Ana threw around had hit the motorcycle club's prized machines. Non-destructive by nature, sinfire differed vastly from hellfire which the demons had deliberately contorted to produce the maximum damage. However, sinfire is still pure source energy and as such it was quite capable of agitating the fuel in the motorcycles' fuel tanks whether intentionally or not.

Anastasia was just reaching for her throwing knife when the first explosion ripped through the courtyard.

It was followed by six more in quick succession, bike parts and burning fuel getting flung in every direction.

The searing heat pushed her back and the concussion wave robbed her of her balance. Using her bad leg to correct herself when she stumbled, a wave of pain surged upward from her stump. Her consciousness waivered and she fell.

Zachary might have seized a chance to capitalise, but he was on fire.

Too close to the motorcycles when the fuel tanks started to explode, the resulting fireball engulfed him.

Was this the opportunity Anastasia needed?

Chapter 35

"We are ready, my lord," announced Adriel, the only female among Beelzebub's generals. She met his eyes when she spoke, then bowed her head as she backed away a pace. Promoted when Nathaniel defied Beelzebub and was killed by the mortal, Anastasia Aaronson, she commanded one sixth of his horde.

Beelzebub wasn't looking at Adriel; not directly at least. He could see her reflection in the mirror he stood before. Standing just inside the entrance of his grand palace, Adriel's legion of demons waited outside.

They did not wait patiently though.

Long had they dreamed about days such as this one. The death curse had always meant they couldn't reach the mortal realm, and even when it began to weaken and they could travel, they had to move with the darkness. They wanted to rule. They wanted to subjugate the humans and punish them for the way they had abused and harmed the planet, but it was impossible to remain in the mortal realm, so until the death curse finally broke, they waited, obeying Beelzebub's command to be ready, but to not waste time teaching the humans what to expect and how to defend against his inevitable invasion.

Tonight though, in response to the actions of the horsemen – who were wildly rumoured to be either dead or locked in Beelzebub's basement – the lord of hell was leading a raiding party.

He knew where Anastasia Aaronson was, and he was going to get the sword and armour back from her. It was his by birth right, and once he possessed it, there would be nothing the humans could do to stop him.

Striding wordlessly from the palace and into the night outside, Beelzebub's enormous frame was all it took to silence the assembled demons.

Halting before them, and taking a few seconds to meet the eyes of those poised to hear his commands, the demons' ruler raised his voice.

"Maximum damage."

His simple order was met with a cheer.

"The humans are developing faster than we expected. As the death curse weakens, so magic is spreading through the mortals. Few have any power worthy of our interest, but there are some who can wield elemental energy in such a way that it may delay or even disrupt our attack when the realms merge, and we unleash hell upon them. Tonight, you will remind the humans how insignificant they are. Kill whoever you wish. Destroy anything you see. But leave Anastasia Aaronson to me."

He turned toward Adriel, a single nod the signal to open the portal. Spies on earth had reported the battle in Mostar, the target for tonight's attack sealed by the presence of the mortal woman wearing Beelzebub's armour.

Attracting yet another cheer, the lord of hell commanded, "Release the leviathan."

Chapter 36

Zachary hissed and seethed, refusing to succumb to the pain as the flames died down. With no hair on his body while in were-wolf form, the burning fuel had found only his flesh to ignite, yet the supernatural nature of his transformed skin meant the fire did little more than sear the outer surface.

It hurt like hell, but stumbling away from the twisted frames of the now destroyed motorcycles, his focus was still on Anastasia.

The sword was back in the sheath between her shoulder blades, replaced by a small knife which she threw at his face. He got a half second to observe the silver thread between it and her hand, then it whipped by his eyes when he employed his lightning-fast reactions to avoid the weapon.

Anastasia never believed she would be able to hit him with it, and worried, in fact, that Zachary might either catch it with one hand, or use the shield to trap it. Either way, it wasn't a serious attempt to end the fight.

It was a distraction.

Zachary thrust off with his left leg. The fight had already gone on long enough and he had been far too generous in letting her live as long as he had. He was going to end it now before Anastasia Aaronson, wanted supernatural terrorist, killed someone he knew.

With his shield to the fore to ensure nothing she did could stop him, he charged.

Hellfire hit him from the side.

Impacting on his shield which sprang to life to protect him, they still carried enough energy to steal his balance.

Stumbling, he twisted his head to find Daniel throwing more hellfire his way. Back on his feet and fully formed, the demon looked several levels beyond angry.

Zachary cursed. The British woman had been stalling, giving her companion enough time to recover. Now he had to fight them both and with the demon in play, the chance of his people getting hurt had just increased dramatically.

The throwing knife returned to Anastasia's right hand, and she threw it again. If she could just stick the werewolf with it, once it was in his flesh, which the magical weapon would surely penetrate, she would hit him with enough sinfire to knock him senseless.

The lightning bolt came as a complete surprise.

"You shall not have him!" raged Gana. Flanked by two lesser wizards, Italian men called Henri and Gino, she was conjuring defensive spells to keep the wounded shifters safe.

Under other circumstances, Anastasia might have applauded the supernaturals working together, but as she picked herself up from the ground, the metallic tang of blood fresh in her mouth again, she questioned if she could beat them all.

The armour protected her from the worst of the spell and reinforced her need to have the shield. Regaining her feet, she swore to take that which she had to have no matter what the price. If she had to kill humans to protect the planet, so be it.

Multiple protagonists faced off against one another, none able to gain a worthwhile advantage.

Daniel threw hellfire at the trio of elemental magicians, causing one to drop his conjuring to raise a defensive shield. Anastasia threw her dagger again, this time aiming to get beneath Zac's shield, but her aim was off, skewed by an air spell, and Zachary flexed his mighty arms, extending his claws in preparation to shred whichever opponent showed the first opening.

The explosion that rocked the city stunned them all.

Chapter 37

The warble of car alarms filled the air before the vibrations they could all feel through their feet died away.

Zachary, Anastasia, Daniel, Gana, and the other supernaturals were trying to kill or maim each other, yet the explosion had been of s-ufficient magnitude to give them all pause. Hellfire orbs crackled in Daniel's hands, ready to be flung, but unused as he twisted his head to the right.

Looking above the buildings at the night sky, he murmured, "That's not good."

Zachary looked at Anastasia. "Was that you?"

Her eyes were fixed on Gana until Zac spoke, questioning whether one of their conjurings might have misfired.

Offering the werewolf an expression that questioned his mental state, she replied, "How could that be me? I'm standing right here."

The car alarms had been joined by sirens as emergency services reacted, plus the sound of a panicked population waking early from their slumber. All those noises were drowned out when a bellow tore through the night air.

The sound was not one a human could make – no one questioned that, but only one of the fighters standing in the ruined courtyard outside the motorcycle club knew what the noise meant.

Drawing in a shuddering breath, Daniel's voice was barely audible when he said, "Oh, no."

The whisper, carried on the wind made everyone else look his way.

"Daniel?" Anastasia questioned. Her body was still glowing with the ethereal light coming from her armour and from the sinfire carried in her throwing dagger. She was amped up and ready for battle, but as if a truce had been called, no one inside their circle of death was trying to do anything right now. "Daniel, what was that noise?"

The demon had his head bowed a little and his eyes were closed. It made him look like he was at prayer. With a tired sigh, he glanced her way.

"A leviathan. An ancient creature and one that Beelzebub has been holding ready for his invasion. They are as close to unstoppable as you can get."

"Wait, did the death curse just fail?" The question came from Gino, a wizard in his mid-thirties. Standing to the left of Gana, he had a fire spell poised for deployment – no one was sure what the rules of the fight were now.

Gana frowned, touching a hand to her chest and looking at Daniel.

She said, "No, I don't think so. I don't feel any different. I think there would be a change if the realms had merged."

Daniel lifted his head though his stance was still one of a person who felt utterly defeated.

"No, it's not the death curse. That's still holding though it seems to weaken by the day. Sunrise is barely more than an hour away now and the tug I should feel to escape its advance is almost not there at all. This, however, is something else."

A second enraged bellow, a deafening sound that made all conversation impossible, followed by the sound of a building being destroyed, ended any possibility that their fight might continue.

Zachary twisted away from Anastasia, exposing his back to her in a move that gave her all the opportunity she needed. For a split second she thought about throwing her dagger, but the werewolf's next question stopped her.

"Just tell me how I kill it."

Daniel sniggered, a deranged laugh escaping his lips. "Kill it? You're kidding, right? You don't kill a leviathan. You hope it finds someone else to kill while you run as fast as you can in the opposite direction."

Zachary flexed his arms. "Not an option, demon. That thing, whatever it is, has to be put down. It's hurting people and you are going to help me stop it." He swivelled on his feet to face Anastasia. "You too, Missy. You claim to have killed demons ..."

"She's not lying," Daniel butted in.

Zachary eyed the tiny woman critically. "Good. I don't know what your deal is, Anastasia, but if you are trying to protect the world from Beelzebub and all that he threatens us with, then prove it. Help me to kill this thing."

Anastasia wanted to reply that she didn't need his invitation to get her involved. That she was doing far more for humanity than he could dream of, but there was no point to discussion. Instead, she reached over her head to draw the sword once more.

Zachary watched the wicked obsidian blade thrum to life with sinfire.

"Hey, Daniel," Ana called. "Want to juice me up?"

Gana and the shifters, many of them beginning to recover from Anastasia's sinfire battering, twitched in fear when the demon formed fresh hellfire. When he started throwing it at the armour-clad woman with the sword, they gasped collectively, but she didn't die.

Quite the opposite.

Before their eyes, the tiny woman appeared to grow in stature and the sword, pale blue light emanating from inside the black surface, slowly changed to red.

Tossing her head to one side to make her hair cascade over her left shoulder, Anastasia grinned evilly.

"Thanks."

The scene was punctuated by a crashing, crunching noise and yet another unnatural, animalistic bellow. Before it tailed off, the lights went out, plunging the streets into darkness. Not visible until that point, the sudden lack of artificial light, highlighted tendrils of white snaking their way across the ground.

They came from Daniel, each attached to one of his fingers, and at the other end, to the shifters still recovering from Anastasia's sinfire blast.

Zachary spasmed when he saw their origin and was about to leap when Anastasia touched his arm. He hadn't seen her move, but she was close enough to place a hand, a prosthetic one he noticed, on his arm.

"He's healing them," she revealed, shocking the werewolf more than he would care to admit. Daniel didn't look their way when she added, "We'll need everyone if we are going to fight that thing."

Gana asked, "You really think we can kill it?"

Daniel released his healing, shutting off the source energy used to repair and rejuvenate the bodies of the shifters. With a nod in Anastasia's direction, he said, "Her sword will do it. If she can penetrate its hide. My worry is that it might not be alone."

Zachary started walking.

"Let's find out."

Chapter 38

I t wasn't exactly difficult to find their target, they simply followed the sound of destruction, yet before they caught up to it, they knew the leviathan wasn't alone.

Rounding a corner with Zachary in the lead only because Anastasia couldn't run that fast, they all saw the demons at the same time. Ana saw Daniel twitch and tensed to grab him if he tried to open a portal. Thankfully, she observed that unlike in Louisiana he appeared to be fighting his desire to run.

In fact, he lifted his hands to fling hellfire and only stopped when Anastasia bumped him.

"Let me," she begged, employing a volume only those closest to her could hear.

She hitched an eyebrow at Zachary and got a comical bow from the seven-foot werewolf.

"Be my guest."

The demons, a small gaggle of them, were a street over from the leviathan. They were blasting at the buildings with hellfire, shattering windows and starting fires. Just ahead of them, a family rushed from a house into the street. Both parents were carrying small children and a third, slightly older child held mum's hand. All bore utterly terrified expressions as the dad plipped open a car.

Anastasia saw when they spotted the demons heading their way. The mortals froze. Not that running would have changed anything.

The demons, five of them, Anastasia counted, were whooping their delight at the sight of fresh victims.

Anastasia's throwing dagger hit the first one in the back of his head which a pulse of hellfire exploded a moment later.

Zachary's eyes flared. "Niiiice." As always, he was looking for Rebecca, and though he hoped tonight would be his chance for revenge, he wasn't going to endanger anyone just to get what he wanted.

The demons had been about to kill the family, and the mortals were being joined by others further down the street as yet more humans fled their homes. The exploding skull got the demons' attention though, as one might imagine.

A second of their number died before they could turn around, and then it became a swift rout as Gana, Daniel, and more lent their effort to subdue the three remaining immortals. Each met their end on the tip of Anastasia's sword, sustained hellfire frying them from the inside to undo the death curse magic that ensured their reincarnation.

As their dust scattered on the night breeze, the group felt jubilant, but their excitement was short lived.

The family of five were still frozen in the street, standing by their car but unable to get their feet to move until the mum screamed. It happened just as shocked cries emanated from the rear of the shifter packs behind the lead group.

The demons they'd found might be gone, but they were not the only threat on the street that night.

Zachary spun around to see what was happening.

"Shilt," he growled. "Easy to kill, but dangerous nonetheless."

It was true that the odd, vampiric, asexual creatures were easy enough to kill, but that didn't apply to normal humans. Humans would have their lifeforce drained by the shilt in seconds, leaving a dried, dead husk where a life used to be.

The real problem with shilt wasn't that they carried a weapon or could kill a person. It was their numbers.

Behind the combined packs of shifters stood a small army of life-sucking supernatural nightmares from the immortal realm. The werewolves nearest were fighting against them, but the shilt had a new tactic.

Launching forward to join the fight, Zac saw as several shilt grabbed a werewolf – one of the Italians, Zac believed, and pulled him through a portal. It happened in the blink of an eye, the creatures taking their prey with them where superior numbers would ensure a successful kill.

Three more shifters were grabbed the same way, snatched from the periphery of the group so fast the pack were only dimly aware of what was happening before their number was reduced.

The initial blow was followed by hundreds of shilt advancing with their weapons, a half metre long stone knife. They cut and slashed, wounding many before the tide could be turned.

Zac flung himself bodily onto a knife that failed to penetrate his skin, swatted the shilt holding it to one side then tore into the tightly formed ranks.

Daniel and Anastasia hit them with hellfire and the three wizards pulled down fire and lightning. The street was awash with ichor as the shilt perished, but the battle wasn't one they could win. Even if the mortals killed all the shilt they could see, there would always be more, and the pack of shifters had been reduced in number by more than a dozen with those taken through portals and those killed outright.

Far worse was the attention they attracted. The lightning, the screaming, the flashes of hellfire bouncing off the low cloud above was drawing more demons to their location.

"There're too many!" yelled Gana. She hated the shilt, the filthy sub-beings plagued the immortal realm, her years there as a familiar had witnessed several attacks on her friends even though the shilt always suffered reprisals from the demons when it occurred.

Anastasia added her thoughts, "We can't fight them and the leviathan! People are dying! We have to tackle that thing head on and stop it. The shilt will follow us and maybe we can find a way to corral them into a kill box."

Zac spun and slashed and ripped through any shilt too slow to get out of his way and he wasn't alone. To his left and right and at his back, the combined pack of shifters were doing just as much damage.

Gana was right though: there were too many and the pack was being steadily whittled down.

Unexpectedly, Zac's shield lit up, bursting into life to deflect an orb of hellfire. Too busy fighting a horde of shilt, Zac was caught off guard and so was everyone else.

Turning to face the new threat, Zac was unable to move fast enough to save Joshua. Hellfire slammed into his body, shunting him back half a metre to fall dead at Antonio's feet.

The pack alpha roared, his rage driving him to attack. Antonio surged forward and would have died too had Zac not thrust his shield out to block the orb coming his way.

Behind the fresh wave of attacks, a pair of demons, both females, were calling for more to join them. There were supernaturals here and that meant fresh familiars if they could be taken alive.

They didn't see Daniel or Anastasia.

Daniel stepped to his right to get a clean line of sight.

"Hello, Victoria," he sneered, blasting her with both hands.

It caused all the distraction Anastasia needed, her throwing dagger whipping across the street to bury itself in the neck of Ashanti, the demon standing next to Victoria.

With a roar of effort, Ana pushed source energy directly through her knife, killing Ashanti where she stood, but the addition to her body count was insignificant.

The pack had no idea how many demons were on the streets. If they had they might have fled, but a sense of how badly outnumbered they were occurred right then as more than a dozen demons appeared from the dark side street behind Victoria just as Ashanti turned to dust.

"She's here, Master! Anastasia is here!" The cry passed back through the demon horde, the message moving too fast to be interrupted.

Trapped in the street, shilt still massing on one flank, Ana, Zac, and the rest now had demons advancing on a second side. They could retreat, but the leviathan they set out to stop was still smashing its way through the city. To get to it they needed to go through one group or the other.

Gana threw all she had at the demons, screaming for Gino and Henri to combine with her as they flung fire at the mouth of the side street.

Daniel pelted the same area with hellfire and Anastasia launched her dagger again, the longer-range weapon proving invaluable. The pack meanwhile had to do their best to hold back the shilt, but they were losing and with nowhere to go an inevitable result was beginning to loom.

Anastasia heard her throwing knife clatter against something metallic – it had been deflected. The flames made the target impossible to see, but as they died down and the wizards switched spells, she saw that nothing they had done had any effect on the demons.

She expected to find scorched bodies, blackened by the flames, but they were largely untouched because more than one was holding a shield of their own. The demons were learning; making note of their recent defeats against the likes of her and Otto Schneider and taking steps to diminish any advantage the mortals held. The shields, a relatively simple conjuring, not that Anastasia could make one, were like tissue paper when compared to hers, but sufficient to stop her knife, Daniel's hellfire, and the wizards' fire.

The ineffectiveness of their offensive and the appearance of yet more demons as they exited the alleyway and spread out on each side caused the mortals to pause.

What should they throw at the demons if nothing had any effect?

Before anyone could find an answer, two things happened.

Chapter 39

Since moments after the first explosion, the sound of first responders, their wailing sirens dominating the night air in the gaps between the leviathan's roars, had been so plentiful that Ana and company had ignored them.

Until now.

With a slew of screeching tyres, police cars powered into sight behind the shilt.

With the street blocked ahead of them, the officers inside did not go slow as one might expect, but chose to accelerate instead. Undoubtedly coming to the aid of the civilian population, they knew the city was under attack from demons and whatever creatures they'd brought with them, so caution had been abandoned in favour of an all-out attack.

It was both incredibly brave and suicidally foolhardy.

With the shilt now dividing their attention between the shifters and the police cars careening toward their rear flank, Ana's focus was still on the demons. They were not attacking and that made her feel very nervous.

Exiting the alleyway, they had peeled off to the sides; left and right in turn to form ... an honour guard! Anastasia realised what she was looking at in a flush of adrenalin-fuelled fear.

From the dark spot between the **demons** at the mouth of the alley, a giant figure strode. Beelzebub, dressed for battle in leather armour that coated his shoulders and left arm, but left his midriff and right arm bare to show his powerful muscularity.

At almost seven feet tall and strikingly handsome, the lord of hell possessed an unruly mane of blonde hair that made him look like an eighties rockstar. In his right hand he carried a long sword that had to be almost six feet in length. It was black like Anastasia's but not lit from within by source energy. Far less deadly than the God Sword, that didn't mean it wouldn't cut a person in half when swung by his hand.

His attitude and stance were relaxed – a leader in complete control of his surroundings.

Once clear of the alleyway and standing at the edge of the pavement some ten metres from Anastasia and her rabble of misfits and shifters, he surveyed the battle scene.

Calmly, he said, "Kill them. Bring the armour to me," and lifting his left hand, he fired a ball of hellfire. It screamed over the heads of the shilt, fizzing with evil intensity until it smashed into the lead cop car, obliterating it.

The burning, ruined carcass of the police cruiser continued forward under its own momentum, thankfully forming a barrier behind which the other cars could find a limited amount of protection.

There was no time for Zachary, Anastasia, or anyone else in their group to see what happened next because two dozen demons let rip with orbs of hellfire.

Zac bellowed, "Get behind me!" pushing the shield and surging ahead to give cover to as many as he could. Anastasia welcomed the hellfire, soaking it in as she too did her best to protect the others.

Even Daniel, unable to fight the terror he felt to once again be in Beelzebub's presence, did what he could to prevent loss of mortal life. His, though, was not an act of bravery, but a calculation of his best chance for survival.

"I'm opening a portal!" he yelled so Ana would hear. "This city is lost!"

Concentrating her effort on Beelzebub, she was in the act of throwing her dagger when she was forced to look around for Daniel.

"No! We have to stay! Gana," Ana sought out the African witch, "can you get the pack to safety?"

With their best efforts, Daniel, Zachary, and Anastasia hadn't been able to protect everyone – another handful of the pack lay dead in the street, cut down by hellfire, or by the shilt when the shifters inevitably had to choose which enemy to fight.

Gana was barely able to think straight. Her heartrate was through the roof and Gino had been killed right next to her in the demons' first volley. He lay right by her feet now and she'd almost tripped over his corpse twice.

Hiding behind a shield when Henri raised it, she pulled on the shilt glove once more.

Beelzebub had watched the first few seconds of the fight with interest. The presence of his father's shield, carried by a werewolf came as a surprise. He'd seen the shifter before, though he couldn't remember his name and it took him a moment to place where the interaction had taken place.

It came to him in a flash as he parried a blast of hellfire from Anastasia. She was hosing the demons with her sustained stream, a technique he could employ himself at any time if he so chose. He preferred to let his horde deal with the mortal, supernatural menace; there would be more battles like this when the death curse fell, and humanity did its utmost to resist his rule.

He knew the werewolf because of Otto Schneider. Beelzebub had seen them together in Bremen and he remembered something else: the shifter was the one who gained immortality when Schneider broke Teague down to his atoms. Both the wizard and the werewolf had absorbed the magic of the death curse that night. It explained how it was that he could be holding the shield now.

A mis-aimed throw by Anastasia saw her throwing knife sail harmlessly by Beelzebub's right shoulder. It missed him as she turned to shout something unheard at Daniel.

Though the dagger struck another demon, who Anastasia promptly dispatched, Beelzebub made sure to catch Daniel's eye and give a quick wink. The traitor might have gained his freedom, but it would be short lived. Unlike his torture, which would go on for as long as Beelzebub could keep Daniel alive.

The police were shooting at the shilt, hunkered down behind their cars, but they were being largely ignored as one might a fly making an annoying noise.

Gana opened a portal, screaming for everyone to get through it.

"Do we pursue, my Lord?" asked Adriel, standing to the left and behind Beelzebub.

He shook his head. "No. Their fear will serve a glorious purpose. They will talk of their defeat and the world will reel from the destruction and death wrought here tonight. Combined, those things will do what we cannot: they will destroy the rising hope."

Zachary had been unable to move as he used his shield to protect the pack. Those who remained, were hiding behind him, desperate to fight, but knowing the consequence if they did. Less than twenty seconds had passed since Beelzebub emerged from the alleyway, and at no point had Zac's eyes left the demon ruler's face.

He had a plan.

It was a stupid plan, but once people were safely away from the danger the demons presented, he was going to enact it anyway.

Slapping Zac on the shoulder, Antonio shouted, "I'm the last one! Come on!"

Zac shook his head. "No, I'm staying. They don't get to win. Get your family home."

"Then what? You think this ends here? We must find a way to fight them! What about the leviathan?"

Zac growled. "I'll deal with that once I've killed these guys." Sensing that Antonio was going to argue, Zac twisted off his left foot and shoved the Italian pack leader backward through the portal.

Gana caught Zac's eye, her face betraying how scared she was.

"Close it!" he shouted, the shilt surging toward him despite the demons throwing hellfire his way. A duo of orbs hit his back, forcing a grimace of pain, but far worse than the torment he endured, he had to watch as another bolt of fizzing, red evil shot by his side.

Having turned away from the demons, his shield was no longer defending their attack. The single orb of hellfire lit Gana's face even as she closed the portal and Zac had to watch as her terrified scream was abruptly cut off.

She had died, her life stolen by the demons as she attempted to escape. The pack had gone through the portal, but that just meant they were trapped in the immortal realm now. Everything he had done had led to this point.

For months he'd been targeting demons, doing everything he could to dissuade them from coming after shifters – his kind – and in just the last few hours, he'd watched the SIA snatch them and then the demons and shilt wipe them out. Those who survived … well, would they ever find their way back to the mortal realm?

Another hellfire orb struck his back, frying his neurons like a powerful electric shock, but this time he didn't even acknowledge the pain he felt. He was too angry. Too bent on maiming those responsible.

Anastasia was keeping the demons back still and had wiped out a fair chunk of the shilt when she switched aim the moment the pack ran for the portal and gave her a clear path to send hellfire their way.

Flexing his arms, Zachary pointed at Beelzebub.

"You. Just you."

Chapter 40

Anastasia knew she was the target. One of them at least. Beelzebub wanted the sword and armour more than anything. He wanted the shield too, and undoubtedly had designs to recapture Daniel now that he was on the playing field.

That Daniel was still with her was shocking; she would have bet money the demon would have bailed the moment the other demons showed up, let alone Beelzebub himself.

Feeling jittery from the expenditure of energy, her arms were getting tired, and the stump of her left leg hurt like hell. Daniel could heal her, but not until they got away.

The wall of demons facing them had been unable to leverage success against a seemingly weaker force only because their master had chosen not to join in. Anastasia had no idea why, and was shocked when he allowed Gana and the pack to escape through a portal.

The why of it was going to have to wait though. Splitting her effort between the advancing shilt, whose numbers were beginning to dwindle, and the demons, just to stop them from getting too cocky, she had to change her tactic when she saw Zac hit with multiple orbs of hellfire.

The shifter had turned his back on the demons – another inexplicable act, but the portal had closed and now it was just her, Daniel, and the giant werewolf with the shield.

Were they any kind of match for the Lord of Hell and his minions?

Mind racing, and with no idea what she was going to do next, she heard Zachary call Beelzebub out.

"You. Just you," the shifter invited, beckoning with the fingertips of one hand like he was Bruce Lee or something. With a twist of his head, Zac looked down at Anastasia. "Get the leviathan. I'll hold them here."

Ana blinked. The demons had stopped firing. Other than Daniel there was nothing worth firing at, and he was once again hiding behind the shifter and his shield.

A shot rang out, the bullet hitting Beelzebub high on his left arm. A dozen bolts of hellfire from the demons to his rear dealt with the final three cops and quiet returned to the city street.

Smirking, the bullet wound already healing, Beelzebub asked, "You wish to fight me, Zachary Barnabus?" Seeing the shifter's eyebrows dance, he added, "Yes, I know who you are. Friend of Otto Schneider, immortal ... for now, because you were there when he tried his hardest to kill Teague. I know about your insignificant efforts to stop my brethren claiming new familiars. You think yourself a champion of the people?" Beelzebub cast his eyes around at the bodies of fallen pack members littering the ground. "You haven't done very well tonight, have you?"

Zachary made a big show of yawning.

"Whatever." Angling his eyes at Anastasia again, he made an impatient face and hissed, "Will you go already? I've got this."

Daniel didn't need to be told twice; he was already opening a portal.

Seeing it, the demons responded with a fresh salvo of hellfire.

Beelzebub snarled, "NO!" but could only watch as Anastasia's outstretched hand touched Daniel's and the pair vanished through his portal to leave a squad of demons facing off against a lone werewolf.

Zac sniggered. "Didn't see that coming, did you, dickhead."

"Dickhead?" Beelzebub repeated, unfamiliar with the term.

The snigger turned into a chortle. "Yes, big boy, your head resembles a penis. Not a big, impressive one though. More like what you might expect to find on a small boy."

Beelzebub hadn't been insulted or challenged verbally in millennia and he wasn't sure how to respond.

"I will destroy you," he sneered.

Zachary made a sound like a gameshow buzzer when the contestant gives the wrong answer.

"I'm immortal, dickhead. Want to try again?"

Beelzebub narrowed his eyes. "I will kill all that you cherish."

He got the same annoying buzzer noise from the giant shifter. Holding up one hand Zachary counted off his fingers.

"Got no family. Got no children. Rebecca killed the woman I liked." Zac paused to look at the line of demons. "Is she here tonight? I might agree to go easy on you, dickhead, if you hand her over."

Angry at the lack of respect, Beelzebub roared, "My name is Beelzebub! I am the rightful ruler of this planet and all who live on it. I will torture you so slowly each minute will feel like an eternity!"

A full-blown laugh burst from Zachary's lips.

"Wow. I am the rightful ruler!" he mimicked Beelzebub, but doubled over unable to keep it up as the giggles took him.

Without warning, he unfolded, launching across the dividing ground to deliver an uppercut with all his claws extended. It was a timed attack, planned and executed exactly as he intended. He was going to end the fight right there and then. The demons might pummel him or even hack him to pieces, he knew, but he would have beaten their lord and master right in front of their eyes and word of that would spread.

Beelzebub would recover; Zachary knew that as he swung his hand upward, but in the battle to come when the realms merged, doubt about the leader's ability to win would damage the demons' cohesion.

It was a shame then that he missed.

Chapter 41

Anastasia held her breath as she fell into Daniel's arms and through the portal. It closed with an audible, yet almost silent, popping sound, and Daniel was already opening another one to get them back to the mortal realm before her heart could find the time to beat again.

With a jolt, she questioned where Daniel might be taking them. She wanted to return to Mostar. Maybe she could kill the leviathan, whatever one of those was, and maybe she couldn't, but she had to try.

However, the sun was going to rise soon, something that always made Daniel twitchy, and it would come as no surprise to find the demon had chosen to take them halfway around the world instead.

A bellow from the terrifying creature answered her doubts before she could voice them, and Daniel released her into a scene of utter carnage.

He could have chosen to open a portal in the creature's wake, or to its flank where she could take a moment to assess what she was dealing with, but to her great shock, they were standing in its path.

Like a dinosaur crossed with a rhino, the leviathan was a creature from a child's nightmare. It had to be twenty feet high and covered in what appeared to be chitinous armour plates like a scorpion. Walking on six legs, articulated at the joints like an insect, it was longer than it was tall by a factor of three or four. The lights were out – power was down across huge swathes of the city, but Ana could see the creature well enough because it was on fire.

Somewhere in the path of destruction, which trailed into the distance behind the enormous beast like a meteor had gouged a path through the earth's crust, one of the many fires the leviathan caused had set fire to the coarse hair that covered its outer shell.

It didn't appear to have even noticed.

Holding her sword with both hands and trying not to freak out, Ana begged, "Tell me there's a way to kill this thing. Is there a weak point on its belly? A flaw in its armour I can exploit using sinfire? A ticklish spot?"

Daniel offered her a forlorn shrug.

"Not that I know of. These things were banished from the demon populated areas before the death curse, that's how long it's been since I saw one. Beelzebub has kept them corralled as ... pets, I guess. Or maybe battle fodder would be a better word. I'm not saying it can't be killed, but he's got lots of them."

"How many?" asked Anastasia, her eyes wide with horror.

"Too many to count."

She swore. A single word she drew out as she considered what tactic she could possibly hope to employ. It had eyes, but they were high on its head and protected by more of the armour plates. Even if she could get to them, would blinding the animal make much difference?

A minivan careened into the street ahead of them, swerving precariously as the driver spotted the enormous beast filling the road. Unable to do anything but watch, Anastasia cried out in hopeless fear when the driver lost control. There was a woman in the passenger seat and for all Ana knew there were children in the back.

The car smashed into a lamppost, stopping it in an instant. Ana's feet were propelling her forward, the desire to help overwhelming all logic and reason. Running to get to the car, she knew she wouldn't make it and had to watch the leviathan's leading foot crush the car like so much discarded junk.

Screaming her rage, Anastasia continued running, ignoring Daniel's shouts as she flung hellfire at the beast's face. Beelzebub, Nathaniel, Daniel ... heck every demon she'd ever spoken to carried supreme confidence they would sweep humanity's defences aside like swatting a fly. Beelzebub had impossible creatures to lead waves of attack, tying up the armies of the world, but what if their confidence was misplaced?

What if she could kill the leviathan? Kill one, learn how to do it and spread the word. That kid she'd met in Louisiana ... Katja – Anastasia had to dredge her brain for a name – maybe she could kill these things with magic. Maybe Otto Schneider could too.

One thing Anastasia knew for sure – she would go down fighting.

Roaring to hide the fear in her belly, she closed the gap, running suicidally at the leviathan's mouth.

A glance over one shoulder told her Daniel had not followed. She was on her own and probably about to die despite the sword and armour.

The stream of hellfire petered out, changing from dark red to light blue as sinfire replaced it. Less destructive but no less potent, Ana continued to blast the creature full in the face as she brought the sword out to her right side.

The leviathan had turned her way the moment she first hit it and bellowed its rage to the sky. Rearing up now on four back legs, it grew another ten feet in height, throwing off her aim and taking away the front leg she'd been planning to amputate.

Would the God Sword cut through the armour?

Dropping the sinfire, with a gasp of determination, she brought her left hand to join the right and swung the sword with both hands as she ran beneath the creature.

It stomped its front feet back down, shaking the ground so hard she almost fell, but the leviathan also brought its undercarriage within striking range.

Now under the beast's chest, she thrust upward, driving the blade between the smooth, flat plates of the creature's underside.

Its screech of pain was like an injection of adrenalin to Anastasia. She had hurt it! Twisting the sword, she aimed to prise off one of the armour plates. That's when basic physics chose to demonstrate how things work.

A lever can turn the world if it is big enough. However, a hundred-pound woman using a sword the effective size of a toothpick against a creature two thousand times her mass and weight can't do diddly.

The leviathan shook its body, trying to remove the annoying barb that appeared to have lodged between two of its armour plates.

Watching from afar, unwilling to get involved, Daniel saw Anastasia thrown twenty feet across the ruined street. Her armour flared into life, protecting her from the worst of the impact, but he could see she was hurt.

He choked back a sigh when she forced herself back onto wobbly legs and swished the sword again.

The situation was entirely hopeless. There was no way for her to beat the leviathan, but he knew she had to see that for herself to understand it – telling her would have been a pointless act serving only to make her want to prove him wrong.

The sun was mere minutes from broaching the horizon now. She was either going to have to come with him or be left here. Either way, he was on a circuitous path to deliver that ultimatum when a whole bunch of portals began to open.

Chapter 42

As Zac's claws swung upward under Beelzebub's chin, the demons' leader loosed hellfire from both hands. The sustained stream of source energy ripped the werewolf's feet out from under him, throwing them backward like they were tied to a truck that just drove in the opposite direction.

He hit the ground out of control, his chin biting into the concrete to gouge a furrow, but Beelzebub didn't let up.

Barrel rolling over and over, the stream of hellfire impossible to fight now that he was on the ground, Zachary was at the mercy of his environment and only stopped when he hit the building opposite.

It then collapsed on top of him.

Finally shutting off the hellfire, Beelzebub turned his head a touch to the right to say, "Go back to the leviathan. The sun will be up soon. I will bring this one with me."

Knowing better than to question his commands, Adriel signalled for the demons to return through the alleyway. It was a short distance to go and there were targets to be enjoyed if they stayed on foot rather than employing a portal to move from A to B.

Beelzebub's eyes were on the pile of masonry that entombed the were-wolf. Beating the giant shifter had been easy and served as another lesson for his horde. Humans were weak. Even the strongest of them. Give them no hope and the invasion would be easy too.

Humanity might even see sense and surrender without a fight. Not that doing so would save them. There were too many people for the planet to sustain and he planned to annihilate ninety percent of them so the earth could recover.

Bending down, he reached into the rubble to find the shifter's inert form.

It was what Zachary had been waiting for.

Slicing upward at the hand – he'd been watching through a tiny gap in the brickwork that covered him – he severed Beelzebub's right arm just above the wrist. It caught the demon by surprise just as much as the sweeping foot that took out his legs.

Slamming into the pavement, his right hand missing and unable to produce hellfire, Beelzebub rolled to his left and away to gain space before flicking himself up and onto his feet.

Zachary tore his way free of the building's debris, to snarl defiantly in his opponent's face as he followed his initial attack with a succession of devastating blows.

Slashing, punching, gouging, Zac laid into the ruler of the immortal realm with more viciousness than he'd ever employed before. When Beelzebub attempted to defend himself with hellfire from his left hand, Zac slapped it away, raking his claws at the demon lord's belly only for Beelzebub to spin away and out of range.

Holding up his remaining hand to ward the werewolf off, Zachary was about to launch a fresh offensive when he realised he could hear laughter.

Beelzebub was laughing.

"Pathetic." The demon shook his head. "Utterly pathetic." Holding his severed right arm out to one side, he demonstrated his mastery in manipulating source energy by rebuilding his missing hand in the space of a heartbeat. "You could make a fine familiar, Zachary Barnabus, but your foolish overconfidence renders you incapable of worthwhile service. I shall torture you until the death curse fails and then watch as you die."

In a blur of motion, Beelzebub came at Zachary, blocking the werewolf's swinging right hand and converting his grip to twist the arm until it snapped the shoulder from its socket. A punch to the throat, a roundhouse kick to the inside of Zac's left knee to drop him followed swiftly by a knee to the face.

Zachary parried with his left arm, looking for an opening only to have Beelzebub smash the arm away with such force the limb went numb.

Reeling and off-balance, Zachary couldn't stop the demon from spinning around his body. In a wrestler's move, Beelzebub gripped Zachary around the shoulders from behind, lifted the werewolf from the ground and into the air to then throw him down with might and gravity to land on his neck.

His vertebrae shattered, paralysing Zachary instantly. The death curse magic worked to fix his severed spine, but unable to fight, there was nothing he could do to stop what would happen next.

Chapter 43

D aniel gawped. Angels spewed from the portals. Dozens of them. Converging on the leviathan, Daniel could only watch in stunned awe as they pelted the creature with sinfire and elemental magic.

Anastasia, her head ringing from being thrown into a wall like a ragdoll, was confused at first as to what was going on and had to look down at her own hand as she tried to figure out where the sinfire was coming from.

When a hand clapped on her left shoulder, she jerked and spun, almost driving her sword right through Serena, Beelzebub's mother and one of his staunchest opponents.

She was just as beautiful as the last time Anastasia saw her. The tiara she wore then was gone, but the hair and clothes were much the same – elegant, flowing, and hardly the thing to wear into battle.

"Come with me, Anastasia," she invited. "Let us get you to safety." She took Anastasia's hand - unresisting in her confused state - and began to open a portal.

"No!" Ana snatched her hand away. "I have to stop that thing!" Lifting the God Sword once more, she sucked in some air, but with the will to charge once more into the fray, the sense of futility she felt kept her feet from moving.

What could she do against such a creature? Saved from the leviathan stomping her into the ground by the arrival of the angels, Ana could see a multitude of them throwing everything they had at the giant beast.

Their efforts had halted its progress, but she could perceive no visible damage to its impenetrable hide.

Twisting her feet to face Serena, Ana asked, "How do we beat it?"

Serena looked apologetic but there was no comfort in her words.

"You cannot, Anastasia. Even you, a demigod, do not have the power to prevent what is to come."

Anastasia had a question in her mouth, but it died as she repeated what Serena had just said.

"Demigod? I'm a demigod? Is that why I can wield the sword?" she asked, casting her eyes down to the obsidian blade she held.

Serena smiled like a parent might to a poorly educated child.

"Yes, my dear. I cannot explain your parentage, but my husband, like all men of power, was wont to stray when the chance arose. It was four thousand years ago, but my best guess is that you are a direct descendant of the same line from which Beelzebub and Godfrey were born."

Trying to do the math in her head while a battle raged behind her, Anastasia stuttered, "I'm ... I'm their sister?"

Her question brought amusement to Serena's eyes.

"No, child. You are far too removed by thousands of generations to be considered a relation, but I believe their father's genes have lain dormant in your family line until the weakening death curse caused you to ... evolve."

Anastasia fought to find words. Everything she had been questioning about her uniqueness had just been explained. She could create a stream of source energy and wield the original supreme being's weapons because she was a demigod.

It was a little much for her to take in.

Exhaling deeply, she murmured, "I need a lie down."

Serena held out her hand again. "Come with me. The sun is rising, and I must leave. You will be safe with us. We can heal you and protect you. Perhaps together we can find a way to stop Beelzebub from his destructive plans."

Tempted, but hesitant, Anastasia said, "But you also plan to rule over mankind. Godfrey's plans are little different from his brother's."

"Oh, but they are. Beelzebub will reduce the human race to manageable numbers through genocide. Godfrey will allow the people of his realm to live their natural lives, managing the reduction in your numbers over generations of carefully reduced breeding. You must see that either one side or the other will win. Your choice is only which one to back."

Serena held out her hand again, beckoning that Anastasia take it.

Wearily, Ana glanced at the leviathan. Had it even noticed her attack? With the sword and armour and the angels at her side, could they defeat Beelzebub?

With a heavy heart, she turned to look at the queen of the immortals and took her hand. Passing through the portal to return to Heavane, her last thought was a question.

How had Zachary fared?

Chapter 44

Hiding from the angels, Daniel saw when Serena approachedAnastasia. Should he go to her now, snatch her quickly before he lost her to them?

He'd known the truth about her heritage … suspected at least, for some time. No one else could do what she did, not even Serena. The only figures in history who could produce a sustained stream of source energy were the supreme being and his direct male descendants. Generation after generation, they ruled because they were the most powerful.

Now standing before Serena was a mortal woman who could do the same thing. The angels would want her just as dearly as Beelzebub. That she had once been bound to him almost made him laugh.

The sun was coming; it couldn't be more than a minute or so from rising. He had to go now – the pull to escape it was too great to resist, but he had enough time to bounce through a portal and grab Anastasia first.

"NO!" the shout of shocked denial sprang from his lips when he saw Serena open a portal. Anastasia was through it before he could react and stunned for a moment he stared at the spot where she had been.

It was the arrival of the demons that snapped him back to reality.

Adriel – he remembered her well, as he remembered her ambition, led them into the ruined street. The demons began blasting at the angels who, caught briefly by surprise, soon returned fire.

The leviathan roared, angered by the sun's arrival. Watching from his vantage point, Daniel saw the creature's outline shimmer. It was being sucked back to the immortal realm, forcibly removed by the advancing sun. His own hand was doing the same when he looked at it.

With no choice in the matter, he opened a portal. If he didn't pick where he entered the immortal realm, he could end up anywhere when the death curse sucked him back there and that was too big of a risk to take.

Stepping out of the mortal realm, he breathed a sigh of relief. However, a final glance at the ruined city of Mostar and the demons he could see still fighting against the tug they must feel to throw one last hellfire orb at the angels, he saw what was absent just as his portal closed.

Landing in the immortal realm on a high and remote hill miles and miles from anywhere, he sucked in a deep breath and opened a fresh portal back to Mostar.

It was perhaps the dumbest thing he had ever done, but the attack on Mostar had awoken once again the acceptance that the humans were going to lose. The humans were going to lose. The angels were going to lose, and there was nothing anyone could do to stop Beelzebub tracking Daniel down and making him pay for his treachery.

He couldn't fix the things he had done, but he could continue in the same vein and lose on his terms.

Stepping into the street where he'd last seen Beelzebub, Daniel found the Lord of Demons picking the battered werewolf's near lifeless form from the ground.

With a grin, he shouted, "Surprise, dickhead!" and fired a glowing orb of hellfire right into the side of Beelzebub's head.

Daniel's former master shot sideways, dropping Zachary as his whole body left the street.

Falling backward through the portal to escape the sun, Daniel snagged the werewolf's arm and pulled.

Beelzebub hit the ground and rolled. His own body was beginning to shimmer, the effects of the death curse dragging him away from the sun. Snarling with furious vengeance, he looked up in time to see Zachary's hand, his middle finger extended, vanish through the portal before the sun's rays hit the street and the immortal realm reclaimed him.

Chapter 45

Colt Ironbolt set the empty crystal tumbler down on the leather coaster on his desk. It had contained several fingers of neat whiskey a few moments ago. Despite the fact that it wasn't even nine in the morning, he gave thought to having another.

Retiring to his home last night to leave the SIA division across the globe to conduct his orders, he'd expected to arrive in his office this morning to be greeted with jubilant news about how many new supers his force had been able to recruit.

Forcibly recruit, yes, but recruit, nonetheless. The world needed them. He could see that, and it was his job to deliver what the world needed.

Except there was no jubilant welcome. Instead, his driver was denied entry to the SIA Headquarters and when he argued with the Marines guarding the gate, he was sent away.

Not that he left. Oh, no, he stood his ground and argued.

That was when the President phoned him.

Ayla Pendragon was to replace him as head of the SIA.

While Colt Ironbolt slept, around the world the SIA divisions either revolted, refusing to obey his command to seize supernaturals from their homes and off the street, or they carried out the order with disastrous consequences. More than fifty people had died, and he was being blamed.

Him.

Colt Ironbolt.

The leader of the SIA and the saviour of the free world.

Not only was it not his fault that people had died – that was the incompetence of those carrying out his orders – more importantly, there was no way to win this war without sacrificing some soldiers. What did they expect? For everyone to make it to the end alive?

"Ayla Pendragon," he spat the name, squeezing the crystal tumbler in his hand as if it were her delicate neck. "How can she replace me?"

No one could replace him. Not so far as he was concerned. His sights had been set on victory and the upswing in popularity he would gain in its wake.

He was going to be president. Global President perhaps after he had united the world to defeat the demons. Well, he wasn't going to be denied.

Rising abruptly from his chair, Colt Ironbolt's thirst for power found a new direction.

Maybe the demons were going to win after all. The news was covering nothing but the story of a massive strike in Croatia. A city called Mostar had been flattened by a horde of demons and a huge creature that looked part scorpion, part dinosaur.

Ironbolt didn't care; the deaths there had no impact on his life.

If he couldn't lead the humans to victory as the head of the SIA, perhaps he could aid the demons. He knew things, intimate battle plans and defensive measures that he felt sure the demons would see an advantage to knowing.

Visualising Ayla Pendragon kneeling before him when the demons rewarded him with a nation to rule – that would be his demand – he straightened his tie.

Getting even was going to be so delicious.

The End

Author's Notes:

H ello, Dear Reader,

It is a sunny afternoon in late August and for once I get to finish a book during daylight hours. Of course, that happened because I didn't stay up last night to finish it.

The characters in the Realm of False Gods, as I am sure you know, are among my favourite. Anastasia's indomitable will and refusal to compromise strike a chord in me – it was the spontaneous creation of her character that gave life to this series in the first place.

Originally, she was going to be a detective solving crimes using magic that came to her because of the piece of shrapnel in her brain. That concept was scrapped early on as the story grew arms, legs, and other characters.

Zac popped into existence when I needed a comedy element to play alongside the serious German wizard, Otto Schneider, and here's a little secret – Otto Schneider is a name from my past. I used to manage the supply chain for a big engineering company. I won't bore you with details, trust me, it's boring, and Otto Schneider was the name of a firm in Germany from whom I bought many millions of pounds worth of product.

When I chose to set the wizard books in Bremen, a city I frequented when posted to Germany as a soldier, I needed a name and that one presented itself.

Mostar is a city I saw during the Bosnian war in the early nineties. The war was done by the time I got there, but the destruction left behind was far from gone, and it stuck with me, surfacing again when I needed a location for the shield.

I mention tear gas, otherwise known as CS gas, in this book. As a soldier I got to experience its effects most years. Sometimes more than once a year as they taught us to take care of our gas masks and appreciate how effective they were. The drills always involved taking the masks off to feel how potent the gas could be in concentrated quantities.

I don't miss the army.

In the past, I have suggested the series might run to twenty books, but it was always a guessed at or notional figure based on some of the ideas kicking around my cavernous head. Now, I suspect we are nearing the end.

In my mind I can feel the death curse weakening. The stage is set, the humans don't stand a chance, but among them are one or two special people who will die trying to save mankind.

The next book will focus on the SIA training academy where Katja, the sisters, and others are honing their skills under Otto Schneider's watchful gaze. It's not going to be a softer story though – blood is going to run.

The end of the world is nigh, but when the dust settles, who will rule the planet?

Take care.

Steve Higgs

What's Next for the Realm of False Gods?

Demon Horde Gambit

Otto Schneider isn't the kind of guy who bothers to seek permission.

The demons have withdrawn from the mortal realm, the attacks have ceased, but while humanity dares to hope they may have gone for good, the irascible German wizard knows better.In the face of overwhelming odds, he's going to do the dumbest thing possible ... attac k.In the wake of the destruction in Croatia, Otto is taking the fight to the demons and he's not going alone.It's a stupid strategy, but that doesn't mean it won't work.But there's a player missing from the board. Where is Anastasia?Now residing with the angels, the human demigod is forced to explore her new status. Whose side is she on? What part will she now play in the battle to come? And why is Godfrey still so confident of victory.While elsewhere Otto and friends fight for the future of humanity, Anastasia learns a shocking secret that may change everything.Other Serie

Raider and Rapier

Graveyard Gods

The currents sweep east, but the dead float south. This corpse laden tide carries with it the destinies of a tomb raider, a knight turned captain, and an empire fraying at the seams.

A grave robber who dabbles in the alchemical arts, Edmond Mondego has spent the last seven years in search of a God Grave. He hopes to find magic within to relinquish his murdered wife's soul to the land of the living. What he finds instead is an imprisoned goddess stripped of her power but in full possession of divine secrets, including a rumor: every five years, one living soul is returned to the Emperor of the Gilded Islands.Meanwhile, the Lord Captain Augustin Mora, newly appointed commander of His Imperial Majesty's Ship Intrepid, guards the forbidden waters for his Emperor. Edmond's profane plundering of a God Grave and the machinations of the admiralty send Augustin on a quest to capture the tomb robber. But an enemy from his past muddies the waters, and Augustin is forced to reunite his old knight's guild and put hand to hilt once again.And so, Edmond sets every ounce of cunning and guile to raise himself through the ranks of nobility, evading Augustin Mora and all manner of assassins; he has only one goal—to convince the Emperor to use the magical boon for his wife's soul, and, failing that, to take the throne for himself.

<u>**More Books By Steve Higgs**</u>

Blue Moon Investigations
Paranormal Nonsense
The Phantom of Barker Mill
Amanda Harper Paranormal Detective
The Klowns of Kent
Dead Pirates of Cawsand
In the Doodoo With Voodoo
The Witches of East Malling
Crop Circles, Cows and Crazy Aliens
Whispers in the Rigging
Bloodlust Blonde – a short story
Paws of the Yeti
Under a Blue Moon – A Paranormal
Detective Origin Story
Night Work
Lord Hale's Monster
The Herne Bay Howlers
Undead Incorporated
The Ghoul of Christmas Past
The Sandman
Jailhouse Golem
Shadow in the Mine
Ghost Writer

Felicity Philips Investigates
To Love and to Perish
Tying the Noose
Aisle Kill Him
A Dress to Die For
Wedding Ceremony Woes

Patricia Fisher Cruise Mysteries
The Missing Sapphire of Zangrabar
The Kidnapped Bride
The Director's Cut
The Couple in Cabin 2124
Doctor Death
Murder on the Dancefloor
Mission for the Maharaja
A Sleuth and her Dachshund in Athens
The Maltese Parrot
No Place Like Home

Patricia Fisher Mystery Adventures
What Sam Knew
Solstice Goat
Recipe for Murder
A Banshee and a Bookshop
Diamonds, Dinner Jackets, and Death
Frozen Vengeance
Mug Shot
The Godmother
Murder is an Artform
Wonderful Weddings and Deadly
Divorces
Dangerous Creatures

Patricia Fisher: Ship's Detective Series
The Ship's Detective
Fitness Can Kill
Death by Pirates
First Dig Two Graves

Albert Smith Culinary Capers
Pork Pie Pandemonium
Bakewell Tart Bludgeoning
Stilton Slaughter
Bedfordshire Clanger Calamity
Death of a Yorkshire Pudding
Cumberland Sausage Shocker
Arbroath Smokie Slaying
Dundee Cake Dispatch
Lancashire Hotpot Peril
Blackpool Rock Bloodshed
Kent Coast Oyster Obliteration
Eton Mess Massacre
Cornish Pasty Conspiracy

Realm of False Gods
Untethered magic
Unleashed Magic
Early Shift
Damaged but Powerful
Demon Bound
Familiar Territory
The Armour of God
Live and Die by Magic
Terrible Secrets

About the Author

At school, the author was mostly disinterested in every subject except creative writing, for which, at age ten, he won his first award. However, calling it his first award suggests that there have been more, which there have not. Accolades may come but, in the meantime, he is having a ball writing mystery stories and crime thrillers and claims to have more than a hundred books forming an unruly queue in his head as they clamour to get out. He lives in the south-east corner of England with a duo of lazy sausage dogs. Surrounded by rolling hills, brooding castles, and vineyards, he doubts he will ever leave, the beer is just too good.

If you are a social media fan, you should copy the link below into your browser to join my very active Facebook group. You'll find a host of friends waiting there, some of whom have been with me from the very start.

My Facebook group get first notification when I publish anything new, plus cover reveals and free short stories, but more than that, they all interact with each other, sharing inside jokes, and answering question.

f facebook.com/stevehiggsauthor

You can also keep updated with my books via my website:

g https://stevehiggsbooks.com/